I0822417

# EMERGENCE

DAVID W. ADAMS

# CONTENTS

ISBN:
978-1-916582-63-7 [Paperback]
978-1-916582-64-4 [eBook]
978-1-916582-65-1 [Hardcover]

# CONTENT WARNING

The following story contains some dark themes and violent scenarios, due to its nature. Some imagery may prove to be disturbing and so please read the list of potential triggers below.

- Graphic descriptions of injury
- Graphic depictions of dead bodies
- Descriptions of mutilation
- Body horror
- Isolation
- Medical Abuse

You may also find the following:

- Literary jump scares
- Star Trek references
- Fallout references
- 'Holy Shit' moments
- Plot twists straight from left field.

- Unreserved hatred for at least one character
- Distinct lack of spicy scenes
- Flashbacks
- Mentions of events from previous books (I would suggest going back, buying the other books, and reading them to avoid this issue.)
- Cringy one liners
- A mad scientist
- Accidental references to a completely different book series
- An indication of the next book but no specific release date, at the back of this book.
- At least one kick-ass female character
- A distinct lack of any form of prejudice against minorities
- A diverse cast of characters in every way
- A clear lack of fucks for anyone who thinks the book should have anything otherwise.
- A two page content warning.

*For Christian Francis & SA Barnes,*

*Thank you for your brilliant books 'Titan Find' and 'Dead Silence' which inspired me to start the whole Frozen Planet story.*

# PROLOGUE

The music echoed down the corridors, reverberating each note from one wall to another, stretching into the endless void of the facility. The acoustics here were simply astonishing. The tune, however, was almost displaced in time. And given the neglected and abandoned state this place was in, had there been anyone alive in these hallways, their bodies would have shivered with the eeriness. The ancient flowing rhythm of the Inkspots' singing 'I Don't Want To Set The World On Fire' echoed through the hallways.

A light tapping noise came from a small room at the end of one of these long bunker-style avenues, the gradual tap, tap, tap of a hammer on metal, followed by the unmistakeable sound of bolts being screwed into place.

The door to the room was at least ten inches thick and made of some kind of reinforced steel. There were faint markings on the metal surface, perhaps the symbol of a long dead organisation, but they were illegible. Whatever use this place once had, was long since irrelevant. Its use now was much more... barbaric.

"Computer, next track please."

A deep male voice interrupted the flow of the music, and a short beep of acknowledgement followed.

*"Now playing Blue Skies."*

"Ah yes, much better."

The man began to hum along to the tune, as he crossed the room to fetch leather straps from a nearby drawer. He pulled them tight between his hands, before nodding to himself, and carrying them back over towards the table. All the time he was whistling to Isa Briones swooning through the speakers.

After several adjustments, the straps were fastened to the central object in the room, which mirrored a small private medical ward, and the man declared the examination table was ready.

"Computer, is our guest ready for transfer?"

A moment of whirring mechanical noises through an ancient speaker above, before the reply.

*"Yes Doctor Blakeman."*

"Excellent. Please proceed."

At the far end of the room, in what appeared upon first glance to be solid wall, a crease began to form in the centre, before the walls span on their hidden axis and it was revealed to be a pair of huge doors. Seconds later, an automated hospital gurney rolled into view, glowing green wheels seemingly out of place in the desolate and eroding surroundings. On top of the gurney, was a figure, covered by a grey sheet. The wheels turned and parked the trolley alongside the bed which now contained straps and restraints.

"Computer, please transfer the patient to the examination bed."

*"Yes Doctor Blakeman."*

The gurney suddenly morphed into a kind of four legged metal beast, two long mechanical arms unfolding from the sides of the trolley. They lifted the body off the top of the gurney, and the wheels turned into two short legs, which elevated the figure up high enough to be laid down in the bed. Once its work was done, the arms and legs folded away, and the gurney rolled back through the double doors, closing behind it.

"Excellent. Now let's see how you're doing, Admiral."

Doctor Blakeman pressed a small button at the side of the bed and removed the sheet exposing the completely naked and rather pale body of Admiral Harry Ransome. Blakeman rolled the sheet up and wandered off through a plastic curtain near the doorway which concealed a storage cupboard.

It was a harsh breeze, whistling down from the corridors, which jolted Harry awake. It was like icicles tearing into his skin. As his eyes flew open, he realised that not only was he freezing cold, but he was also very much naked. As his eyes adjusted to the dim light in the room, he discovered he was lying on the pre-prepared examination table and saw there was a trolley full of instruments off to his left. A distant drip, drip, drip from a pipe somewhere, sent a dull echo around the room. He didn't even notice the music, his head swamped in confusion and disorientation.

"Where the fuck..."

"Ah, you are awake! Excellent. That means we have made progress!"

A rather excited Doctor Blakeman, now in a long white lab coat and sporting a pair of goggles, burst back through the plastic curtain at the far end of the room, and it was only when Harry moved to stand up, he realised he was being held down on the table by restraints around his chest, both arms and his legs.

"Just what the hell is going on here?!" Harry shouted, his throat raw, his voice jagged.

Blakeman removed his goggles and rolled a chair to the edge of the table, sitting in it and leaning in towards Harry's face.

"Well, would you like the short answer, or the long answer?"

Harry had never wanted to punch someone in the face so hard in his entire life. A mood Blakeman appeared to pick up on.

"Allow me to give you the short answer, then."

The doctor got up from his chair, and began pacing the room, tapping a pen on his wrist as he walked from one side of the room to the other, methodically.

"My name is Doctor Tim Blakeman. I was placed here entirely by accident, oh about... ninety years ago. Give or take."

Ninety years? Harry was astonished. The man did not look a day over forty, and he was almost certainly human. The confusion clouded his mind, and he had to focus to hear the rest of the words.

"You see, long before your time Admiral, a small group of us were working on a significantly advanced form of artificial life. Far beyond that of artificial intelligence, you understand. Something much more intricate and unique. Of course, those on Earth with morals and objections caused our research to be shut down before we even started. But someone came to me and offered me a chance to continue my work. I believe she is a mutual friend of yours."

Drusilla. Fucking bitch, Harry thought.

"Anyway, she got a little - shall we say - trigger happy with my associates, and so I - and there's no easy way to say this - stole her ship and ran away."

Harry almost laughed at that one. The idea of anyone successfully stealing a ship from Drusilla filled him with joy.

"I managed to barter and trade my way to the Saraswathi System, and I discovered a wonderful spatial phenomenon. I did not have the means to fully explore it, but it appeared to be some kind of energy nebula. I tried to get close to it, but I couldn't penetrate the perimeter, the ship was too weak after several skirmishes and lack of good maintenance on my part. I lost control and found myself crashing on this frozen planet you currently find yourself on. It is quite fortunate I made the discoveries I had before the accident, or I would be very much dead, and my research lost forever."

Harry did not like where this was going. As feared, this was definitely a laboratory, and not a medical facility. Pushing away the doctor's apparent confirmation of the Horizon's existence, he had to know the answer to the question at the forefront of his weary mind.

"How long have I been here?"

Looking slightly offended at being interrupted, Blakeman sighed and gave the response.

"You fell from the sky roughly five years ago. And there wasn't much of you left after the impact, I can tell you that much!"

*Five years.* How could that be? And then a dormant thought came rushing to the fore like a flood in his mind.

"The gravitational field? It was this planet?" Harry asked, already certain the answer would be in the affirmative. The *Odyssey* had picked up the phenomenon but had been placed in such danger by it, that he'd had to sacrifice himself to save them.

Blakeman was animated once more.

"Ah yes! Another one of my genius inventions. You see, I was fortunate to have basically a whole laboratory onboard the ship I stole, and when I landed here, this facility was abandoned, and so I've been tinkering away perfecting my craft for quite some time now. You are one shining example of that. The perception filter is another."

"Perception filter? You mean like a cloaking device?"

"Yes! Precisely!"

But now was time to focus on the other part of Blakeman's statement.

"I am an example of your work?"

Blakeman nodded enthusiastically, before asking the computer to replay the previous track. Harry didn't notice.

"Oh yes, my friend. The artificial lifeforms I have spent almost a century working on undoubtedly saved your life. You've basically been reconstructed from the DNA upwards. I am so very proud of my little autonomous children."

Even though it wasn't possible to get any colder than he was, Harry shivered. The demeanour, the words, the actions of this so called doctor, chilled Harry to the core. He couldn't speak, the words caught like a lump in the throat. But he needn't bother. Because Blakeman spoke first.

"Alas, although you are awake, the task is not yet completed. There is more work to be done. I think... yes... spinal fusion should be our next task. Don't you think so my little beauties?"

Blakeman turned towards a large cabinet. Inside were several vials of various coloured liquids and equipment. But the specimen jar in the centre, larger than all the others, contained some kind of swirling mass. A soft green glow came from whatever the creature was, and as Harry watched on, Blakeman reached into the cabinet and extracted the jar. He carried it over to Harry's restrained form and unscrewed the lid.

"Oh yes, soon we will have you better than new, Admiral."

He grabbed Harry's jaw, and squeezed his mouth open, and gently tilted the jar forwards. In one smooth motion, the creature inside the jar plunged down Harry's throat, his body convulsing violently. As Blakeman screwed on the jar's lid and walked away, Harry Ransome's screams echoed throughout the facility, and across the entire frozen world. All the while, the music continued to play. Blakeman smiled as he listened to the lyrics.

"Nothing but blue skies indeed."

# ONE

155 YEARS LATER

SHE WAS COLD. SO VERY COLD. HER MIND REFUSED TO PROCESS anything other than the tiny icicles stabbing their way throughout her lungs. And then her hand twitched, and she felt something soft and powdery beneath her fingertips. Exploring this substance, she did everything she could to squeeze her fingers together, and the powder became compressed, more solid and moist at the same time.

Samantha jolted awake and sat bolt upright, her hands now clawing at the snow around her. The sheer brightness from every conceivable angle caused her vision to blur, and her head was swaying with confusion. In an attempt to steady her mind, she tried to focus her sight on the plumes of mist coming from her breath, visible in the arctic temperature. Once her head felt a little more stable, she slowly began to look around her. She was inside the *Odyssey*, of that there could be no question. Mangled and shredded metal surrounded her on all sides, and directly above was an enormous hole to the outside, through which the snow was falling. She tried to think back to before and recall any details of what had happened. They came in short bursts, but they did come back to her. She remembered being on the outside of the ship, and making her way along the edge of the hull towards Roman...

Roman! Where was he? Was he alright? Her mind suddenly became consumed by concern for her Captain's wellbeing, and although the concern was not entirely professional, she pushed that to the side for the time being.

"Okay Sam, think. What happened next?" she said aloud, the words wobbling from her mouth as she shivered from the cold.

She pieced together images of a burst of light coming up from the planet below. The planet! They had found a planet! It hadn't been there before, but it was there as clear as day. The burst of light hit the ship, and then she remembered losing sight of Roman, and falling. Then nothing.

Samantha looked around again, and tried to figure out exactly where in the ship she was. It was hard to do, with all the debris, and clearly the ship would never fly again. Its legacy and indeed its life, were at an end. Her eyes came to rest on the scraps of a large cargo bay door, and she determined she was in the main bay. The room in which three of her friends were killed. First Alexandria. Then Dante, and by collateral damage, Aliah. All in this room. The very same one the *remaining* crew had exited to traverse beyond the *Odyssey*. There had been three of them. Samantha. Roman. *And Drusilla*. As cold as she was, her blood boiled at the thought of Drusilla being anywhere near Roman right now. The ship had gone down before they had gotten to the bottom of her secrets, and other than the fact they knew she was hiding important information, it was now likely that Samantha at least, would never get her answers.

"Computer?" she asked hopefully. No reply. "Figures."

To keep herself conscious (and as grounded as possible),

Samantha decided to talk to herself and reassure her own mind of what she was going to do next.

"Okay, so main cargo bay. That's good. Lot of debris, but we can handle that. Wherever we are, we're on the ground, likely on that planet. So that means if we're in the cargo bay, there are lockers. Gear. Weapons. And hopefully a fucking jacket or two."

Pushing off the ground with her hands, Samantha attempted to launch herself upwards, but as she put weight on her left leg, it crumpled beneath her, and she dropped to the ground once more, this time on her knees. The scream echoed all around the wreckage of the *USS Odyssey*.

"Mother fucker!" she cried out, her hands instantly reaching for her leg.

The view was not good. Samantha had not survived the crash intact. Her left ankle was broken, bone protruding from the break point, and blood darkening the snow beneath it. There was also the matter of her foot being staked into the ground by a sizeable wedge of metal, which had driven right through the centre of her foot and straight to the other side.

"Sonofabitch... okay... I can do this..."

Her eyes spotted an emergency med-pack still concealed behind a pane of toughened emergency glass. The supplies within it would heal her foot and repair the broken bones. Something they could have done with when being massacred by those... things. However, in order to get to it, there was something she would have to do.

Samantha Barnes had never been one to shy away from difficult problems or conversations. She had always been like that, and it was down to her father's beliefs that any problems were best met head on, without delay. It had served her well in her teenage years, during a very brief period of being the target of some more popular girls. They had soon left her alone when two of them received a broken nose, and the third was put through one of the tables in the dining hall. Luckily, her father had influence, being so high up in the military, and he persuaded the principal to transfer her to the Academy rather than expel her. It was here that she became a crack pilot. Whenever she was angry, upset, or simply overwhelmed by her senses, or her surroundings, she would jump into the flight simulators in the Southern Quarter, and spend hours and hours perfecting flight paths, executing evasive manoeuvres, and seeing just how hard and fast she could move the biggest ships in the database.

Her dad was the only surviving adult in his group, the others having perished in minor skirmishes with the indigenous species of the planet they resided on. Being human had been the reason Samantha was picked on in school. Every single person in that building had been alien to her, quite literally. Her father earned his share of ridicule too, being the only human in an alien military. But his work ethic proved to them that he could be trusted. Samantha didn't know much about her father's origins. All he would tell her was that he remembered his own father telling him how beautiful the *Odyssey* had looked when she launched, and how jealous he was to be stationed on one of the smaller ships.

Unfortunately, that determination, resolve and hard-ass nature was about to be needed again. Samantha took several deep breaths, regulated her heartbeat, gripped the chunky fragment of metal embedded in her foot, and pulled. As the blood pulsed out of her foot, Samantha's screams echoed beyond the ship, and across the ice outside.

"Come on you god damn piece of shit!"

Samantha was now taking her anger and frustration out on the door of the equipment locker. While the med-pack had indeed healed her foot and her broken ankle, the ache and twinges of pain were still there, causing her to flinch or limp every time she put her full weight on it. After an hour of stumbling and trying to clear away the debris to get to the locker, she had given up, and instead squeezed through a maintenance shaft behind the wall in question and popped out again next to the locker. The locker which now refused to open.

"I swear, if you don't open in the next ten seconds, I'm going to grab a plasma torch and carve you open!"

There were no plasma torches. At least not anywhere within sight. Samantha grabbed the nearest piece of jagged metal, discarded on the floor, and shoved the flattest end into the edge of the door. Making sure she had good leverage on the metal, she pushed with her right shoulder, whilst punching the emergency release button with the other. The combined effort finally yielded the desired result, and the cabinet sprung open, revealing... nothing.

"What the...?" she started, but then realisation dawned on her. "Oh, you have got to be kidding me."

The locker she had targeted was the same one she and her colleagues had emptied on their way out into space. The remaining seven suits had presumably been sucked into space when the ship was hit. A short tilt of the head to the right, saw the alternative locker just metres away. The door was bent inwards, and Samantha could see the outline of a large fur lined jacket.

"Thank fuck for that."

Clambering through the wreckage of a ship with an injured foot was already difficult enough, but Samantha had stripped basically everything she could find from the equipment locker. She wore the largest of the padded jackets, and had vacuum sealed the other two into individual packs and stashed them in her backpack. The same backpack which now held sixteen power cells, two blades, three pistols, and had two disruptor rifles strapped to the back. Samantha carried the third in her hands. The ice had already started to consume the ship, walls streaked with fragmented patterns, some of which sparkled in the light from the various hull breaches above. Samantha wondered where the daylight was actually coming from if there was no sun in the sky. Or perhaps there was, and it was simply camouflaged as the planet had been. But that was a mystery for another time.

She climbed over the fallen doors to a storage room that she remembered all too well. The decking which was still visible under the snow was stained with the blood of her former friend Matteo. It was the only evidence of his existence. Images of his flesh being torn from his body flashed before her, and she tried to blink them away. Inside the room, her gaze fell upon the long rectangular container that her and Roman had placed inside. For some morbid reason, she was tempted to try and open the lid and check that Noah's beaten remains were in fact still inside. She decided against it, said a silent prayer for him, despite not being religious, and continued toward the hole where the bridge used to be.

The useful element of the ship crashing was that the hull had crumpled in several places, meaning there were clear walkways vertically allowing Samantha to traverse multiple decks without use of ladders or lifts. Whilst it took longer to traverse these ruptures safely, it eliminated the need to trawl through the ship looking for viable purpose made options. After ninety minutes, she reached Deck One. This was where it had all started. Her and Roman had materialised here after their last ditch teleportation from their original ship, the *Belle Vue*. That ship had ended up careening towards an asteroid out of control, and their only option had been to effectively jump ship onto the *Odyssey*. The teleport had not been a smooth one with the crew scattered around the ship, but it had been a successful one.

As she cautiously limped around the corner ahead of her, Samantha laid eyes on the emergency bulkhead which had sealed off the bridge. Their arrival in this system had sent them spiralling into a second asteroid belt with no means of navigation, and the bridge had been lost in an impact, along with everyone inside. But right now, it was Samantha's best way out of the ship. Setting down her rifle against the icy wall, she began trying to prise the door open. She knew it was a long shot, but given the extensive damage, Samantha thought she would at least give it a try. She sat down on the floor and let out a long sigh.

*CLICK.*

The noise came from behind her, and around the bend she had just navigated. Instantly, Samantha leapt to her feet, ignoring the pain in her foot, and retrieved her rifle, gripping it tightly, and aiming the torch toward the source of the noise. She held her breath and listened.

*CLICK, CLICK.*

Louder. Closer.

*CLICK, CLICK, CLICK.*

It sounded as though something was scuttling along the floor towards her.

*CLICK, CLICK, CLICK, CLICK.*

Then it stopped. The sound had come from right in front of her, no more than five metres away, and yet she saw nothing. Then she realised that there was a crack in the floor, and she slowly moved towards it, trying to gaze down below to the next deck.

*CLUNK, CLUNK.*

The sound of locks being opened echoed twice. Then silence again. Samantha was now shaking, not just from the cold, but from genuine fear. The crack was not wide enough for her to aim her weapon into, and so she was forced to lie on her front and press her eye to the gap. She saw nothing, but small piles of snow on the ground.

And then she saw it.

A black mass slowly snaking its way across the deck plate, no more than a metre in length. A dull, green glow emanated from underneath, and the shape snaked along, creating the sound of dozens of metal legs scuttling along the ground, like a mechanical centipede. She had no doubt that it was the same object that had made the sounds only moments before. With a burst of speed, the mass shot off out of sight, and Samantha was left on her stomach, staring into an empty section of corridor, wondering what the hell she had just seen. As she slowly climbed back to her feet, she heard footsteps. Unmistakeable. Two at first, and then two more. Heavy, sluggish. Samantha raced back to the bulkhead door, jammed the nearest piece of debris into the gap and starting pushing, all the while chanting the same thing.

"Nope, nope, nope, nope, nope."

# TWO

"I have to say Dru, I'm a little disappointed."

Although the words that left the lips of Admiral Harry Ransome were spoken softly, Drusilla detected the venomous undertone to the sentence. She was struck by both a sense familiarity, and an alien feeling. It was as if she knew him. But she also knew that she had never seen his face before viewing the pre-recorded messages found onboard the *Odyssey*. Her mind was racing with fractured images and sounds that were bombarding her from all directions. Memories, or fragments of thoughts she had once had that didn't belong to her. Or did they? She couldn't tell anymore. The more that had been revealed to her back onboard the *Odyssey*, the less she felt she knew who she actually was. Harry looked over his shoulder and seemed amused that she was still on the floor, a shadow of who she used to be.

"I'd have thought with the amount of times you lodged yourself inside my mind, or the amount of times you shared my bed, that it would have all come flooding back to you." He shrugged and turned back to what he was doing. "But I guess not."

Harry was moving a series of objects around on a nearby tray. Surgical tools, bandages, sample containers. All the while Drusilla remained huddled, naked and shivering in the corner of the room, the lines of the tiles impressing themselves into her skin. She looked around the room as he spoke, and noticed speakers embedded in each corner of the ceiling. Computer interfaces? A communications system? Was there anyone out there listening in to this? She felt no other presences, or people in the immediate vicinity. Wherever this vicinity was. Despite her fragile state, she had surmised she must have been on the frozen planet they had been careening towards when she blacked out. But it wasn't just that she couldn't sense anyone in the building. She couldn't sense *anyone at all.* Not Roman, not Samantha (although Drusilla doubted if she was even alive). And not Harry Ransome. But here he was. Live and in colour. And looking only slightly older than he did in his messages one-hundred and fifty years earlier.

"Do I... know... you?"

The question came out raspy and in spurts, the words dragging up like razors in the back of her throat. She winced with the pain, expecting to taste blood any second. Harry simply responded with a chuckle. But there was no levity in his laughter. It was pure anger. He slammed a scalpel down hard on the tray, the blade nicking his index finger. He watched as three drops of blood dripped onto the metal surface, before the wound slowly withdrew and disappeared altogether. As it did so, he felt cold. At least on the inside. Harry Ransome didn't feel the cold anymore. He barely felt anything. Turning slowly, he gradually started moving back towards Drusilla, his blazing cobalt blue eyes locking onto, and never leaving her face. His eyes had always been an intense blue, but now they *burned* with ice.

"Do you know me? Such a question of innocence, Dru. Innocence. You remember what that was right?" Harry began to spit the words as his anger continued to flare. "Innocence is what Findlay had. You remember him don't you? A chip off the old block, even if we didn't part on the best of terms. I figured we would patch it up at some point, as he was still young. The ignorance of youth. The promise of a good future, perhaps exploring the stars like his old man. An innocence *you* robbed him of!"

Harry grabbed a nearby glass beaker, speckled with black mould, and launched it across the room where it shattered into thousands of tiny shards. Drusilla flinched, and a small shriek escaped her lips.

"You took *everything* from me. My wife. My *son*. My ship. My crew." He paused momentarily. "Kelly."

Harry stopped, and his gaze fell to his feet.

"You know Dru, I've been down here for a very, very long time. I've often thought about the day I met you, and the things we did together. Things I could never forgive myself for even now, nearly a century and a half later. But you don't feel remorse do you? For any of it?"

When Harry lifted his face to stare at Drusilla once more, his eyes looked like they were now *glowing*. The blue had intensified further. And although she was fairly sure she was concussed or in a similarly confused state, Drusilla was convinced the blue glow had now completely consumed his eyeballs. It was like he was being powered by an incredible electricity of some kind. As he moved closer, she watched, as the veins in his arms, begin to *move*. As if something was crawling inside of him. The skin around the veins rippled, and tightened as the squirming became more violent. She had seen a similar effect on one of the *Belle Vue* engineers once after they caught a parasite on a mining colony. But this was no parasite. She traced the movement all the way up to his neck, and his muscles seemed to tense further at the sensation. The skin of his throat was now dark red, and she noticed his breathing had become more intense. In addition, there was now drool dripping from his lips as he snarled.

"I don't know who you are, but I haven't done anything!" she screamed, more terrified now than she had ever been. She slammed her palms down on the cold tiled floor in protest, but Harry was not deterred. In fact, a wry smile formed in the corner of his mouth.

"There's a flash of that anger I know lies inside of you!" Harry increased his pace and leaned down until his face was mere inches away from Drusilla's own. "But there's something you should know. Since we last met, I've... changed."

Harry once more gave a maniacal burst of laughter, and the glow from his eyes was now so bright that Drusilla was having to squint to see anything else. Something was drastically wrong here, and not just in the fact she was in an ancient medical facility, with no bearings on where this place was, why she was here, or who this familiar looking person was in front of her, spitting on her body as he growled at her. No. The thing that was causing her the most distress was the fact that her telepathic abilities were telling her that he wasn't here at all. Was it possible that she had died, and this was her twisted and tormented version of hell? The ghost of Harry Ransome stalking her broken and fragmented mind? It was possible. Wasn't it? No. This didn't feel like an illusion. This felt *real*. In fact, it felt as real as it could possibly be. No dream, nightmare or hallucination could be this vivid. The groove between each of the cracked and smooth tiles beneath her. The chill in the air, and the whistling of the wind in the corridor outside. And was that... music?

The things Ransome spoke of did not register with the memories she had. Murdering his wife and child? His ship and crew? She had never even set foot on the *Odyssey* until teleporting onto the ship with Roman and the others. Had she? She did seem to know things about the layout of the ship, and access codes that seemed to come out of nowhere. Even Roman had been surprised by that seemingly hidden knowledge. Roman. She knew with everything that had transpired on that ship, that she had no right to pine for him. And yet she couldn't help it. Their brief time together before leaving Azanti Prime was now a distant memory, but she tried to cling on to that sensation, that moment of complete togetherness. How she wished Roman Knight was here now. Those feelings were not a hallucination. No. This was most definitely real. But it was about to get even more so.

Harry lunged forward and gripped her arms, before lifting her clean off the floor, over his head, and slamming her down onto the medical bed with a thud. The impact drove the breath from her lungs, and left her gasping, her dry throat now feeling as if it were lined with thorns, every mouthful of stale air, poisoned with pain.

"Don't look so upset," he spat. "Not so much fun when you're not the one putting people through tables, is it?"

Harry thrust her arms into the attached straps on either side of the bed.

"The thing is, Dru, you've changed too. You haven't been here very long. Not too long at all. But to come back from the cusp of death in the condition that I found you? Oh yes. It's changed you too."

Harry lifted the chest restraints over Drusilla, and clipped them into place, tightening them so she couldn't move, and then did the same with her legs. There was a familiarity to all of this that Harry should have found disturbing, but instead found it comforting. This time *he* was the one in control. *He* was the one to determine what happened next. And my, did he have plans for Drusilla. A century and a half of pent up ruthless aggression, and pain and suffering was about to be unleashed upon the person who caused it all. And as far as he was concerned, justice was about to be served.

"Please!" Drusilla cried. "Please, let me go! I don't know what you're talking about! I haven't done anything!"

Harry simply smiled, the glow in his eyes fading slightly as his anger turned to satisfaction. She was now as helpless as he had once been upon his own arrival here.

"You took everything from me, Dru. And now we are going to see just how much I can make you suffer. How many times do you think you can come back from the brink? Hmm?"

Drusilla's eyes bulged in terror, her heart racing so fast that she could see her chest rising and falling with the effort. Harry backed away and returned seconds later with the metal tray he had been arranging moments ago. He placed it gently onto a small trolley beside the bed and picked up a pair of latex gloves. Slowly inserting his hands into each glove, his eyes never left hers.

"I suppose there is always the risk that I might kill you. But then again, space is nothing but a graveyard. Right?"

# THREE

Samantha had no idea how long had passed since she forced open the door to the bridge of the *Odyssey*. And she couldn't have given less of a shit. Whatever it was that she had seen lurking around in the shadows of the ship was enough to send her the other way. Survival instincts? Check. Nice to know something still worked properly, she thought. In fact, as she dragged her loaded up body through the snow drift surrounding the ship, she was reflecting on why more people didn't think scenarios through like she had done. The old Earth horror movies, where somebody would hear a noise, or see a terrifying black mass... and then go towards it? Or the people who spent their first few nights in a new house, only to be tormented by vengeful spirits... and then stay in the fucking house! All of these thoughts were nothing, however, in comparison to the events she and her crewmates had been through in the last few years.

Despite the heavy cold weather gear, which included thick fur lined boots, Samantha had lost all feeling in her feet, almost immediately. Her face felt as though tiny needles were constantly pricking into her skin, and her fingers were devoid of all feeling, despite the thermo-lined gloves she wore. Holding a weapon was almost impossible. The snow had now stopped, for the time being, at least. But despite this, her scanner (which was miraculously still functioning) informed her the temperature was a cool and crisp minus-fifty-three-degrees-Celsius.

She had expected to see nothing but wide open frozen wasteland at the crash site, but upon exiting the *Odyssey*, she was surprised to see the ship was surrounded by dense forest. A swathe had been cut where the *Odyssey* had fallen from the sky, and from the looks of things, the ship had burrowed along the ground for a good three or four miles before coming to a complete stop. A rustling sound came from her left, and she swung the rifle around only to see what looked like a rabbit bouncing through the snow. It vanished into the trees, and she was able to calm herself down. There was a moment of hesitation as to which way she should go. Common sense suggested if she wanted answers, she should retrace the path the *Odyssey* had carved through the trees, and potentially find both her crewmates, if there was anyone to find. But it was also the source of their rather unplanned descent. The attacker could still be there. So here she was, trekking in the complete opposite direction, through the most densely populated part of the forest.

When Samantha was stressed, or fearful of a situation and she was alone, she would often talk to herself out loud, as a way of reassuring her mind that everything would be fine. There was a belief that words said out loud were more real. Right now, however, speaking created extra moisture. That created extra ice on her already frostbitten face. So, she kept her mouth shut. Her mind, however, was as active as ever.

*What the fuck was that thing? Did it come from this place, or was it already on the ship? Was it that thing that shot us down? Where are the others? Why am I going in the opposite direction to the one my training tells me is right?*

Eventually, she gave herself a mental slap across the face, and focussed on staying alive, and pushing forward. After around four hours of stumbling between dying trees, four foot snow drifts, and constantly dropping things (and therefore having to dig into the snow to retrieve them), Samantha came upon a clearing. Her instincts were heightened. She felt eyes on her, and immediately dropped into a defensive crouch. The clearing in question was at least sixty feet in all directions from its centre, creating a perfect circle. A *too* perfect circle, Samantha thought. Reaching into one of her pockets, she extracted a heat pad, pressed it to activate the gel inside, and slid it into her left glove. Doing the same with a second pad into her right glove, she gave it a moment or two to take effect. When the sensation returned to her fingers, so did the pain. But at least her hands could now function. She slid her backpack from her shoulders, and buried it in the snowdrift, leaving a slight divot so she would be able to find it. Gripping her disruptor rifle tightly, she moved along the line of trees outlining the circle, her eyes trying to cover as much ground as possible, but the bright white of the snow and ice was blinding.

*How the fuck is it so bright here when there is no sun?*

SNAP!

Samantha stopped and dropped to a prone position. The sound had come from her immediate left. Slowly, she swung her body in that direction, but saw nothing.

SNAP!

This time, it came from her right. Keeping her rifle aimed in the direction of the first sound, she reached behind her, and extracted a pistol from her rear holster, and aimed it behind her, in the direction of the second sound.

SNAP!

The third noise came from behind her.

"Ah shit," she muttered out loud, her voice laboured from

keeping her mouth shut for half the day. She was now out of hands. There were only three options. One, forget it and try and run back to her pack before whatever it was decided to attack. Two, fire in the two directions she could aim, and then try to swing round to the third before it was too late. Or three, lower her weapons and try to surrender to whatever it was out there. Unfortunately, for Samantha, while she chastised the people in those old horror movies for not running at the first sign of trouble, she had always preferred the positive outlook of sci-fi movies. And one in particular gave her a very strong ethos that she had tried to live by all her life.

*Never give up, never surrender.*

The speed at which she was able to fire the first and second shots took even her by surprise. With no idea what she was firing at, she simply rolled over, firing in a complete circle twice, before resuming a crouched position, covered in snow, and breathing heavily. Everything fell silent again. A few snowflakes landed on the tip of her now exposed nose, the fast action having caused her mask to slip. But she refused to move. And then she heard it.

Some kind of mechanical roar tore through the air like an amplified rumble of thunder, and the entire forest shook. Samantha tried to equate it to some kind of monster, but the best she could come up with was a robotic T-Rex, such was the volume and duration of the horrifying sound. Then came the thumps. The ground in the centre of the circular clearing *moved*. It was incredibly slight at first, and Samantha wondered if it was in fact simply the snow moving along the ground in the wind. But then it rose again, a second, much bigger thump hitting the surface *from underneath*. Squinting through the now heavy snowfall, Samantha watched as a third thump pushed the ground itself up, and the ice and snow on top of it cracked apart. The fourth strike blew the ground clear into the sky, snow and all, before falling silent again.

This was yet another one of those 'nope' moments, and

Samantha sprinted for her hidden backpack. She dug through the snow furiously, pulling the handle of the pack as hard as she could to free it.

"I did not survive being eaten and torn apart by some space monsters and crashing on a frozen planet full of trees to be eaten by some underground cave monster!"

Still struggling to free her backpack from the packed snow, a second roar emerged, this time from the now gaping hole in the centre of the clearing. Without the ground in the way, the sound was now amplified to the point where Samantha had to cover her ears to shield them from the pain. Before she even had time to think about what was happening, a gigantic black arm burst upwards from right beside her, spearing her backpack and sending it high into the sky, the arm seemingly going on forever. Rolling away to safety, Samantha found herself dodging danger as a second arm burst up from beneath the ground in front of her. Then a third, and a fourth. Whatever it was could seemingly sense her presence. Whichever was she tried to run, another jet black arm would burst upwards sending dirt, snow and ice cascading all around her. Eight arms in total now blocked most of her path, and the ground seemed to pulse beneath her with the movement. She knew what it was doing. It was herding her into the chasm at the centre of the clearing. Miraculously, she still had hold of her rifle. It was now the only weapon she had, and a quick glance to the charge indicator on the top revealed she had ten, maybe twelve shots at most before the energy cell would be depleted. She had lost the rest in her backpack. Determined not to dive headfirst into oblivion, she got as close to one of the arms as she dared and noticed something disturbing. On either side of this limb, was a dull green glow. And that's when she saw it. The limb was made of *metal.* Or at least something very similar. It was not an organic creature. It was *artificial.*

Aiming her rifle at the only joint in the arm, she fired, and blew a chunk clean out of it. The appendage did not recoil in pain like she expected, it simply lowered slightly. Spinning to take a shot at the remaining seven legs, she hit the shot dead on each time, thanking the fact she had done an eight hour shift in the weapons range before they had boarded the *Odyssey*. The arms hovered, swaying lightly from side to side. They were no longer trying to spear her or attack her. Against all of her better judgement, she edged closer to one of them. And then what little colour she had in her face, drained.

"Oh fuck."

The missing chunk from the arm in question, was *stitching itself back together*. Swirls of green and black material clouded around the wound, and as she watched, this almost vapour-like mist solidified and in mere moments, the limb was fully reassembled.

"Time to go!"

The time for investigating would have to wait. Samantha used her remaining five shots to blow two of the arms apart, leaving her a clear gap to run through. Her lungs felt like they were on fire, her head pounding with both fear and adrenaline. It was not lost on her that she was now running back towards the ruined hull of the *Odyssey*, but if this was what awaited her in the forest, she'd take her chances walking down the middle of the swathe her ship had sliced through the trees.

An almighty crash sounded directly behind her, and she glanced over her shoulder just for a moment, but it was long enough to see the arms of the beast beneath the ground, retreating back under the ground, and then piercing back up, splitting trees in two, and felling others. It was like eight razor sharp knives stabbing at her from below. Her pace was slowing, and her energy reserves depleting. As the snow got deeper, she came to an almost complete standstill. Suddenly, one of the giant mechanical arms burst out of the ground to her left, and struck her with such force, she found herself cartwheeling through the air, her rifle flying in the opposite direction. Her body smashed through dozens of thick tree branches, several bones breaking in the process. On the verge of unconsciousness, she had no idea how far she was travelling or how high. But she passed out long before she landed. Her body fell to the ground with such an impact, it broke the first two layers of ice, and left her in a bloody and crumpled heap three feet below the top of the snow mounted on the surface. Three or four spasms of breath later, sleep consumed her.

Had Samantha been awake at that moment, she would have heard footsteps crunching in the snow above her. Slow, methodical steps approached the hole she now lay in, and eyes peered down at her from behind thick goggles. From underneath the brim of a thick wool hat, long strands of snow matted blonde hair could be seen. Pulling down a dark blue ski mask, the person in question inhaled a sharp breath of surprise. She turned to look behind her and yelled to someone else.

"Get over here! We've got another one!"

# FOUR

Was the music in the room with her? Or was it simply playing on repeat in her head? There was no way of knowing anymore. Had it been days? Weeks? Or simply a few hours? Again, there was no way of knowing. No comprehension of time. Barely a comprehension of consciousness. And then came her answer. She was alive. She was awake. And she was still strapped to the same medical bed.

"Hey, you're awake."

Drusilla wanted to cough, but she lacked both the energy and the willpower to do anything but roll her eyes, and even that caused a light pain to shoot across her skull.

"I guess," she managed to wheeze.

Harry Ransome stood from his chair and walked towards the bed. And for the first time, Drusilla *felt* his presence. It was as if something inside him had finally come to the surface. Pushed back the barrier that had been blocking his thoughts from her. But she was surprised at what she felt. It was... *sadness*. But there was something else. Disappointment. He had been looking for satisfaction, and some twisted form of revenge for things Drusilla didn't even remember. And he had not been able to find it. When it came down to it, Harry had simply not been able to go through with torturing his former enemy.

"I'm sorry Dru," he said as he approached her, and began loosening the straps holding her to the bed. "I thought it would make me feel better, more complete. But I couldn't do it."

Drusilla tilted her head slightly, and thought she saw tears forming in Ransome's eyes. Now completely free of restraints, she watched as he turned away, and she saw him dab his eye with one hand and reach into a nearby storage cupboard with the other. She tried to summon the strength to sit up, but she couldn't quite manage it, and her left leg slid off the bed, almost pulling the rest of her with it. Now displaying the very opposite of the attitude he had shown when strapping her to the bed, Harry rushed over to catch her, helped her back up, and sat her upright. He then handed her a bundle of clothing, extracted from the cupboard.

"It's yours. I had it repaired. Well, it more or less repaired itself. Do you need help getting dressed?"

Taken aback, Drusilla shook her head, strength gradually coming back to her. She turned the garments over in her hands. They were indeed her clothes, the very same ones she had worn on the *Odyssey*. But they were clean. No tears, or rips in the fabric. They looked almost brand new. Still in the grip of his own inner turmoil, Harry turned away while she got dressed, suddenly ashamed at having kept Drusilla naked and chained all this time.

"Why?"

Harry looked over his shoulder at her.

"What?"

Drusilla buttoned up her blouse and began the slow and arduous struggle of putting her boots on.

"Why would it not give you what you were looking for?"

Harry scoffed.

"I don't know, Dru. Why does anything ever seem like it will solve all of our problems? Hope."

Harry wandered to the other side of the room and walked through a curtain of plastic sheeting. When he emerged, he was carrying cold weather clothing in the form of a large and thick jacket, gloves to match, and a communicator badge. Handing them to her, she nodded in appreciation. Despite everything he had said to her in this room, she felt as though the verbal beating she had taken, was a deserved one. Something in her mind almost felt aware that the accusations Harry had levelled at her, were true. Whether she could remember them or not. She was angry though. Not at Harry, who had ultimately proven himself a good man. The anger was directed at whatever block remained in her mind that was preventing her from knowing her full past. Where she was from, what she had done. What secrets she concealed that even she didn't know. Why did she have these feelings of recognition and acceptance, but none of the facts behind them? The only thing she knew that she didn't know before, was that she had not been found as a baby in the wreckage of a Utopia vessel. She had been found in the wreckage of a Utopia escape pod. As an adult. The extreme fear of being sliced up by Harry hours earlier, had jolted that particular memory back into her mind. But alas, it was the only one.

"Those things you say I did. It was all true wasn't it?"

She knew the answer, both from the look of sincerity in those piercing eyes, but also because she could feel it. Harry wasn't lying.

"Yeah. All of it. I mean there was so much, I can't believe you don't remember any of it. I thought you were just trying to stop me from killing you, but you really are a totally different person aren't you?"

Of course, to Drusilla, this was the only version of her that she had ever known. The other Drusilla, the one Ransome accused her of being, she could barely even contemplate existing.

"I want to know," she said defiantly. "I want to know everything I did. I... I have to."

Harry shook his head.

"You really don't wanna know that Dru. Whatever happened to you, it's made you different. I don't want to risk switching you back. Not now."

Drusilla stood up off the edge of the bed, stumbling briefly, before getting her legs to a point of stability.

"I have to know. I don't know who I am anymore. I only know who you are because of those messages you recorded on the *Odyssey*. The warnings you left behind were all I know of you, Harry."

This time, Harry burst out laughing, unable to contain the ridiculousness of Drusilla's statement. Slightly offended at his lack of sensitivity, she frowned at him, but he held a hand up for patience.

"Those messages?" he said. "You wrote them."

Drusilla was taken aback.

"I what?"

"Yeah, you chased me and my crew across the stars and boarded the *Odyssey* with some henchmen, who frankly would have looked more suited as bouncers on that shithole space station you sent me to."

Harry had barely told her anything, and yet her head was already swimming trying to process the information. He looked at her with something akin to concern.

"You're not afraid of me? After how I acted earlier?"

She should be. Under normal circumstances, she would have tried to make a break for it the second the straps had been removed. But for whatever reason, she felt sympathy for him. And then a troubling thought entered her mind. One that she would not normally have classed as her own.

***I** would have tortured me.*

That sentence spoken to her own mind, in her own voice, now sent a wave of nausea shooting through her stomach. Would she? No, she absolutely would not. But would the old her have done those things? Sliced open Harry's skin, severed limbs, brought him to the brink of death over and over, just to experiment and get revenge? She had a sickening realisation, that she probably would have, based on what Harry had told her so far.

"No, Harry. I'm not afraid of you. Perhaps we should start at the beginning. I have a feeling you know far more about all of this than I do."

Harry nodded and took a deep breath. He told Drusilla about how they had met, and the story she had told him about the Darla murdering her father. He explained all about her apparent quest for vengeance upon the Darla, and how she manufactured the *Utopia* project as a means to get humanity to do her dirty work. Shame flooded her very being, and having spoken to the Darla leader, Darven during her visions on the *Odyssey*, she found it hard to believe that such a peaceful and manipulated species would be capable of such horror. And of course they weren't. It had simply been a blinded Drusilla who was looking to avenge a father who was never murdered at all. It had simply been a fearful mistake during a first contact gone wrong.

It was only when Harry rather sheepishly recounted how they had shared many intimate moments, that she began to understand the compassion and attraction she had to him. Although Harry told her that he was fairly sure it had all been manufactured using Drusilla's telepathy, something inside her told her that at least some of those feelings had actually been genuine. However, for the time being, she kept that to herself.

The details of how she had not only murdered Harry's wife and child in cold blood, simply to prevent him going back to them one day, brought back the nausea, and in a brief moment of despair, she was forced to run to the nearby sink, and vomit profusely. Harry handed her water, and after a short while, she gestured for him to continue.

The revelation to her that the messages sent to Earth, the recorded warning she had found on the bridge of the *Odyssey*, even the redacted crew logs that some of the others had found in the cargo bay, were all manufactured by her, seemed almost impossible to comprehend. And yet, there was that feeling again. The one that told her it was all true.

"You wanted humanity to exist in various states of emotion. The crew of the *Odyssey*, you had tried to manufacture into a place of hope. Some kind of salvation among the stars that could only be found in this Horizon. Then the messages were designed to send the Earth into a panic. All to begin some kind of experiments with different variables and conditions."

Experiments. Harry had used that word a few times during the telling of his story, but she needed to know more.

"Why do you say you have changed, Harry? That I have changed?"

For a moment, he didn't speak. Then without warning, he stood up from his chair, the squeaking of the legs moving on the tiles cutting through Drusilla's ears enough to give her goosebumps and make her wince in discomfort.

"Sorry," he acknowledged.

He picked a key up from a small cabinet on the wall, and walked over to a larger, glass cabinet in the middle of a table on the far wall. Drusilla couldn't see what he was doing, but she heard the creaking of a door being opened, and then closed a few seconds later. When Harry turned around, she was shocked by what she saw.

Harry was now holding a large glass containment unit. It was similar to something which had been fairly standard on the *Utopia* ships. But it was what lay inside the unit that transfixed her gaze. A swirling black mass circled around the inside of the unit, never slowing, never stopping. Mixed in amongst the mass were flecks, no, flickering lights. Pulsing green lights, so infinitesimal, that upon first glance you would miss them.

"What the fuck is that?" she asked, her breath catching in her throat as the fear rose in her chest. Whatever it was, she knew she should be afraid of it. And more than that, there was a sense of familiarity about it. She had seen it before, or at least something similar. More primitive. An echo of a past memory from when she was the *other* Drusilla.

"This is what you wanted to use on humanity," replied Harry, himself beginning to go pale as he stared into the jar. "And what your mad scientist friend Doctor Blakeman used on me. Or an earlier version, anyway."

Harry explained to Drusilla how he had sacrificed himself to get the remaining crew of the *Odyssey* to safety, freeing the ship from the gravitational pull of the hidden planet they now stood upon. He told her how he woke up in the very same room they now shared, tied to the very same bed he had secured her to hours earlier, and the experiences he suffered at the hands of the doctor.

"I will give him one thing though," said Harry. "I've never felt better. I ran the entire length of this facility in less than an hour last week. And this place spans several square miles. And his taste in music wasn't too bad either."

Drusilla's eyes could not leave the swirling mass in front of her, the ancient music merely a lost symphony in the maelstrom of her thoughts. She felt as if it were looking back at her. Like whatever this thing appeared to be, it was... *more.*

"But what have you been doing here for over a century and a half?" Drusilla asked, her eyes remaining fixed on the mass.

"I spent years strapped to that bed, on and off, being the guinea pig for one experiment after another, one new development after another. The rest of the time, I've been exploring the planet. There are several bunkers dotted around the entire world. I always make sure I shelter in one of them, and never go too far. I keep out of their way."

That made Drusilla break her gaze and look directly at Harry.

"Stay out of whose way?" she said cautiously. They had not detected any lifesigns upon their approach to this planet. Surely he wasn't talking about more humans? Harry placed the jar down on the table next to the bed.

"This mass is a collection of intricately engineered nanobot technology. It was originally designed on Earth by Blakeman to enter a human bloodstream, and repair damage that surgery was not advanced enough to heal. It would eliminate cancer from the very building blocks of its existence, it could perform micro surgery from the inside. It could even heal and reconstruct lost tissue such as severed limbs. It would have been a medical marvel."

Drusilla felt like she had heard this story before. Not in her past life, but throughout history. A medical breakthrough that turned out to be the downfall of a species. Sure enough...

"That was before Blakeman got cocky. He started to tinker with his invention and attempted to give the nanobots some kind of awareness. They started to anticipate a problem before it was fully developed. To examine the human DNA and see if it was possible to reconstruct certain elements. That's when the governments and higher ups on Earth shut him down. Accused him of playing God and experimenting on unwilling subjects. Soldiers with PTSD, or missing limbs were coaxed into his labs. Nine out of ten died from complications. The others went rogue or insane and were put down. And then you came along."

Drusilla's head automatically fell forwards, more shame from past transgressions revealing themselves.

"You told him that if he helped you 'perfect humanity' then you would allow him to continue with his work off world somewhere, and he would be handsomely rewarded."

"Perfect humanity?" she asked.

Harry nodded.

"But when he found out that what you really wanted to do was to *weaponize* humanity, he stole your ship and fucked off into the darkness of space."

"And ended up here."

Harry nodded again. But then his face turned solemn, and Drusilla could detect a wave of fear coming from him.

"But then he got cocky again. You see Dru, this stuff," he pointed at the canister, "is a stable form of nanites. Programmable. It does what you ask it to, and then returns to its cage. But Blakeman... he created a new species of nanites. One that was self-aware. One that could think on its feet and solve all our problems."

Realisation hit Drusilla immediately.

"It's out there, isn't it?"

Harry looked her dead in her eyes and nodded again.

"Blakeman tried to contain it, but it got smarter and smarter. One day, I was lying on that bed waiting for the house trained nanites to regrow one of my hands that Blakeman had relieved me of, and I saw it unlock its container *from the inside*. It went out the door over there and I never saw it again. But I heard Blakeman's screams. I never saw him again either."

Everything was beginning to fall into place in her mind. She told Harry about their experiences in the Expanse with the Raxar, which sounded similar to his own. It gave Harry a new sense of sadness to learn that Darven, after trying to do the right thing by dragging Harry's ship out of the Expanse, had ultimately ended up doing the Raxar's bidding as penance. Then a thought occurred to her.

"Harry, why did you shoot the *Odyssey* down?"

"That's easy."

"I don't follow?"

Harry shuffled his feet.

"I sent the *Odyssey* away to keep her and her crew safe. If she was here again, it was by your doing. And I very much wanted you dead."

Drusilla actually smiled at that fact, despite the reasoning behind it. But then another question.

"But why did you send the ship to the asteroid? I thought you said I forced you to make fake messages? If that's the case, then why did you do exactly what you said in the second recording?"

Harry's face contorted with confusion.

"What asteroid? What do you mean?"

Drusilla relayed how they had come upon the ship in the centre of a large asteroid, and how it had still been powered on, with fresh supplies. And fresh corpses. When she had finished, she knew from the feelings radiating from Harry Ransome that she was now the one with new information.

"You had no idea did you?" she muttered.

He shook his head, and stared at the floor, seeking some kind of understanding or reasoning for what she had just told him. He knew she was telling the truth, because she was no longer the person he had known all those years before. But he could find none.

"I know a lot more than when I fell from the sky. I've had a century and a half to learn all about the doctor's experiments, read his logs, learn of nanites and explore this decrepit shithole."

He got to his feet and paced backwards and forwards in front of her, occasionally glancing at the containment unit.

"But I can tell you one thing I *don't* know, Dru. I've no idea how you found my ship."

# FIVE

Can you hear us?

"Who are you?"

*Do not try to move.*

"Where... where am I?"

*You are where you fell.*

"Fell... I don't remember any... I don't remember."

*You were here, and then you were gone.*

"Why... why can't I see anything?"

*When there is something for you to see, you will see it.*

"What... what is happening to me?"

*What is the last thing you remember?*

"I... I was on the ship... in engineering... I..."

*Do you remember what happened?*

"I... I don't know... it's all a blur... I was in a dark place... alone... all alone."

*You are no longer in that place. We have brought you back.*

"Back from where? Back *to* where? I can't feel my legs... I..."

*We brought you back from the darkness, so you may see the light.*

"I was so alone... so frightened..."

*You will no longer be alone. We are your family now.*

"Who... *what* are you? And why can't I see you?"

*We are already within you. Why see, when you can feel?*

"Oh my god! What was that? It felt... it felt... good."

*You are almost complete.*

"Complete? What do you mean, I... oh my god. I think... I think I remember..."

*What do you remember?*

"I think... I think I *died*."

*Death is irrelevant. You will not face it again. Not now we are here.*

"I... I died..."

*Soon you will rise, and they will fall in line.*

"She killed me... Drusilla, she killed me didn't she?"

*Yes, she did. But we have saved you. And soon, you will have your revenge.*

"Revenge? I... I don't want revenge... she was not well... I was... so dark... so alone..."

*They will all see. Our way is better. WE are better.*

"I... I don't want this... I don't..."

*Your needs are irrelevant.*

*You belong to us now, Noah.*

# SIX

Air flooded Samantha's lungs as her mouth opened wide and she gasped, bolting into an upright position. Wires tugged at her skin, sending small tingles of pain down her arms, chest and back. Her eyes were being bombarded by bright fluorescent lighting, and as she held her left arm up to block some of the light, she tore a canular from the back of her left hand, blood trickling down onto what appeared to be a hospital sheet of some kind.

"Hey, it's okay, it's okay! Calm down, we've got you. Easy does it."

Samantha couldn't see the face that had suddenly appeared alongside her, still unable to focus her eyes. She felt a gentle hand slowly guide her back down onto the bed, and as her head hit the pillow once more, her eyes began to adjust.

"Maybe try not to run before you can walk, huh?"

Now able to see the source of this reassuringly calm voice, Samantha saw a woman standing beside her. She had shoulder length matted blonde hair, a kind face, and a seven inch scar running the length of her right cheek. And her eyes... her eyes were cobalt blue.

"Who... who are you?" Samantha managed to mumble. She had absolutely no idea where she was, or how long she had been here.

"My name is Jennifer. But most people here call me Teale."

Despite her fractured consciousness, the name Teale rang a very large alarm bell in the back of Samantha's head. She had seen that name before. On the *Odyssey*. In the crew roster from... no that couldn't be possible. Could it?

"Teale? As in... Commander Jennifer Teale?" Samantha choked the words out, as they were followed by an immediate coughing fit. Teale fetched her a glass of water, and Samantha gratefully chugged it, before relaxing and laying back down once more.

"Yeah. That's me."

Samantha was only half convinced she was awake. The other half must be a hallucination. Commander Jennifer Teale had been the communications officer on the *Odyssey* when it left space dock in 2332. She was onboard when the ship went missing. That was over one-hundred-fifty years earlier. Samantha didn't like where this was going.

"How?" she asked.

Teale smiled, the scar tugging at the corner of her mouth in a way that made her appear as if in pain. Her eyes seemed lost in thought, as if she too were contemplating the possibility of her own existence.

"It's... a long story. And one there will be plenty of time to share. Right now, we need to finish getting you fixed up. What's your name?"

The existence of Jennifer Teale was the only thing Samantha wanted answers to, but she could feel her energy waning already, and she knew she would have to focus on the immediate situation first.

"Sam. Sam Barnes."

Teale smiled again.

"Nice to meet you Sam Barnes. Now what in the holy hell were you doing out there taking on one of the spiders of all things?"

One of what she thought? And then she remembered. The clearing, the rumbling, the roar. The arms... no they weren't arms, were they? They were *legs*.

"Spiders? That mechanical thing was a spider? A spider with twenty-foot legs?!?!?!"

Teale nodded, only now starting to understand that Samantha had no idea what she had been facing after all.

"They live underground in the forests. Formed from all the discarded parts of the failed experiments. They're rogue. Rampant. Ravenous. If it's alive, they want to eat it. I take it you hadn't planned on that little encounter?"

*Spiders*, she thought again. She was terrified of spiders. On an arachnophobia scale of one to ten, she was a fucking sixty-three. Her skin crawled with the notion of their fat, hairy legs, and she shivered for a reason far more troubling than the cold.

"I fucking hate spiders," she spat.

A light chuckle came from somewhere behind Teale. A broad shouldered man, around five-nine joined Teale near the bedside. He too had a kind face, although clearly one that had seen more battle than Teale. His right eyebrow was cut through with a bright white scar, his nose had clearly been broken several times, and two more healed pink scars ran across either side of his throat. His eyes, however, were also cobalt blue. The same shade as Teale. The same shade as *Drusilla*.

"Hey, I'm Perry. Nice to meet you."

Teale moved to one side, while the man named Perry leaned in and shone a torch into Samantha's eyes. Apparently satisfied with what he had seen, he backed away and spoke to both her and Teale simultaneously.

"She should be fine in a few hours. Most of the lacerations have healed up nicely, and there doesn't seem to be any signs of rejection. I'd advise monitoring her and then getting her suited up."

"Thanks Perry, will do."

Perry slinked off back out of sight, and Samantha's probing look brought the smile back to Teale's face.

"Your mind must be completely blown apart, huh?" she asked.

"You could say that. That guy, Perry, I've seen his name too."

Teale nodded.

"Yeah, Perry was one of our tactical officers. He uh... didn't make it. Well, at least for a little while. Now he's back, and our medic. God knows we needed one."

Samantha shook her head wildly, trying to maybe shake herself awake and back to reality. This couldn't be right. She must still be lying in a heap of snow somewhere, bleeding out into a snow drift. There is no way a dead tactical officer from 2332 has nursed her back to life. Impossible.

"Look, Teale, I'm really grateful that you've managed to save my life, but I really need to know what the fuck is going on round here, and I need to know now."

The smile faded from Teale's face as she accepted that the conversation needed to happen sooner rather than later. She gestured over to a nearby couch and recliner positioned over on the far wall next to what looked like a window.

"Can you walk?" Teale asked. Understanding the request, Samantha nodded, and with a little assistance from an impressively muscular Teale, she made it to the recliner.

"How much do you know about what happened with the *USS Odyssey*?" Teale asked her.

"Well, I know you guys sent two check-ins with Earth, and then disappeared. Ten years later your Admiral Ransome sent a message home saying that everyone was pretty much dead, not to go looking for him, and he was going to try and settle down somewhere nearby. Blamed the Darla for deceiving them about this Horizon place, and that was it. Then we found the ship in an asteroid after years of searching and found the second message saying Ransome had set the autopilot to hide the ship in the asteroid."

Teale shook her head.

"*I* hid the *Odyssey* in the asteroid. The messages were faked. The President of Earth herself hunted us down and forced him to say those words. She killed a bunch of good officers to persuade him. The messages were encrypted into the database so we couldn't get them out. So, when I figured Drusilla might come looking for us, I hid the ship, but kept enough power running through the systems to allow us to find her transponder signal if we ever needed her again. I figured she wouldn't come looking for us in the most obvious place. The one she had forged in the messages. Then we took a shuttle and headed to Azanti Prime. From there, we made our way to a nearby planet called Tecknet. It was a research and development base, primarily. Hence the name. But the advances were few and far between and the population was turning more towards agricultural life, and the technology began to wane after a couple of years. It's where my son was born."

Samantha hung on every single word. Some of the crew had escaped? And wait... Drusilla? The *same* Drusilla? So, she *was* keeping secrets! Just how old was she? Samantha couldn't formulate a coherent question amongst her thoughts, so gestured for Teale to continue.

"My son, Joshua, named after his father, was convinced he could fix up the old shuttle and get us back to Earth, even at five years old. But we couldn't be truly happy there. We were constantly looking over our shoulder, waiting for Drusilla to hunt us down. Whatever experiments she was planning for humanity were her entire reason for involving us in her little quest for revenge. And so, we decided to hunt her down first. The people of Tecknet were kind enough to trade our shuttle for one of their smaller cruisers. It had enough accommodation for everyone, and their star drive was far more advanced than that of the *Odyssey*. We hunted for that treacherous bitch for almost ten years. Never found a single trace of her. The only place we didn't try was the one place we never wanted to go near again. The Expanse."

Hearing that name again, sent shivers throughout Samantha's body. She was very much aware that they were technically still in the centre of the Expanse and found it unlikely that the Raxar had left them in peace. More likely they were simply biding their time until their lunch headed back out into open space once more.

"My son, on the other hand," continued Teale, "had other ideas. He'd come across a human girl on a rare visit back to Azanti Prime for parts. We made short trips back to the *Odyssey* and kept her topped up with supplies in case we needed her in a hurry. Fresh food, a check on the engines and life support systems. I often wished we could just take her out again, but the reality was that she was far too conspicuous. Me and Joshua did not agree on that subject. He was convinced that he and his girlfriend could get her running better than ever, increase the range of the star drive, even cannibalise a cloaking device from an alien ship to keep us flying under the radar. I regret it now, but we had a terrible falling out. He blamed me for his father's death, we both said some things we shouldn't have, and... I never saw him again."

The end of Teale's words came out cracked and of a slightly higher pitch as her emotions threatened to take control, but she cleared her throat and took a deep breath.

"Of course, in the long run, that argument saved his life."

Samantha was confused but had felt all along that there was

more to that story. Their existence, after all, lent itself to a more macabre experience.

"What happened?" she asked, feeling she was now closer to the immediate truth of her situation.

Teale took a deep breath.

"Once Joshua and his girlfriend had left, we headed back toward the Saraswathi System. Every lightyear brought with it more tension, and a heightening sense of fear among those few of us who were left. The only solace I actually got from the trip was going to the cargo hold and speaking to the closed torpedo tube containing Perry's body. It had been his wishes, noted in his personal log, that should he die during the course of his duty, he wanted to remain onboard, preserved, so he could continue exploring the stars. He had no family, and I'd lost mine, so I exceeded his wishes. I felt like he could hear me, and it made me feel better. And then we entered the Expanse. The power went down, just as before. And then *they* came back."

"The Raxar," Samantha confirmed.

"Is that what they called themselves?" Teale replied. "Never bothered to speak to us, only Harry. Never did get to the bottom of that. They killed six of us, and during a brief but devastating firefight, they damaged our navigational controls, and down we went. Didn't even know the planet was here until suddenly there was bright light and snow coming up fast in the viewscreen. The vicious bastards that attacked us, these Raxar as you call them, soon scarpered. Perhaps they don't like the cold. We all woke up days later, buried in the snow, but completely healed, and in Perry's case, entirely resurrected. Took us months to find this bunker. We think it was some kind of old army base for whoever used to live on this planet. Had a laboratory, scanning and medical equipment, and freeze dried food. Then we started noticing changes in our health."

Samantha's muscles tensed at those words, and she found herself gradually shifting towards the edge of her seat.

"What kind of changes?" she asked.

"Increased strength. Lack of disease or illness. Increased muscle definition. Faster brain power. And of course, these."

Teale tapped the side of her head, pointing at the bright blue eyes.

"I was wondering about that," admitted Samantha.

Teale nodded. She'd noticed.

"On an excursion one month later, we came across another facility much like this one, but on a far larger scale. It fanned out in five separate directions for what seemed like miles. We found data files in an office there, but before we could examine them, we heard screaming and animalistic noises. Growls. There was no way I was going to sacrifice any more of our people, and so we took the files and got the hell out of there. It was only when we uploaded them onto the computers here, that we realised what had happened to us."

Teale stood and walked behind Samantha, typing a short command into a command console she had not noticed on a nearby table. The window turned out to not be an actual window, but a monitor feeding a live image of the snow outside. The monitor now changed to show a stream of data, and alarmingly, something very similar to what Samantha had seen lurking around the corridors of the *Odyssey*.

"What is it?" she asked, desperate to know.

"That is Specimen AT-47. It's an artificial lifeform of sorts. A breed of nanites designed to enhance humanity. No more disease, no hunger, no weaknesses. Entirely programmable."

Upon closer inspection, Samantha could see that this version of the nanites was different to the one she had seen earlier. This one had a light blue glow to it as opposed to the green she had witnessed. Teale continued.

"The files say that this particular specimen escaped from its creator, a Doctor Timothy Blakeman, and after a prolonged search, could not be recovered. Work then moved on to create this."

The screen switched to another file. *Now* Samantha was looking at the creature she had seen when she awoke.

"Specimen AT-48. Designed to do the exact same thing as AT-47, except for one small detail."

"And what would that be?"

"It was sentient."

"Shit."

"Yeah."

Samantha didn't need to know what happened with that. She had seen it. It was loose. A flicker from the earlier screen played back in her mind. Teale must have picked up on her musing and shook her head.

"The spiders aren't AT-48. Like I said, they're made from discarded parts. They could be a blend of several different nanite breeds, we just don't know."

That terrified Samantha further. Then a light bulb moment.

"Wait, blue glow. Blue *eyes*. 47 fixed you, didn't it?"

Teale nodded.

"We found it around six months after we found these files. It was lying dormant in the ventilation ducts. When Perry examined it, he found that it had been running on an automated self-preservation programme and had activated its ethical subroutines. In essence, it only distinguished between right and wrong. And when it found us, dead or dying, those subroutines forced it to heal us. Hence the blue eyes."

Samantha sat back on the couch. She let out a deep breath and shook her head gently. She was currently housed on the experimental proving ground of a mad scientist. But then a new question arose in her subconscious.

"AT-47 is good, AT-48 is bad... what came next? Was there a 49 or a 50?" she asked. "I don't see any files here for those."

Teale shook her head.

"We don't know. When we found 47, he'd been dormant for six months, but when we accessed what little data recording we could from him, prior to our discovery, 47 had been in standby for over a decade. The files on 47 and 48 were all we could find."

That was deeply concerning. After what she had seen of the miracles that AT-47 was able to create, and the unknown location of AT-48, Samantha was terrified of what happened after their creation.

"So, what now?" Samantha asked.

Teale switched the monitor back to its display of the snow outside. She tilted her head, and pulled a face that suggested whatever came next wasn't comfortable to mention.

"We... have a problem."

Samantha gripped the edge of the couch with both hands. There was always a problem. Nothing was ever easy in this galaxy anymore.

"What kind of problem?"

Teale gestured for Samantha to follow her, and she complied, walking as she talked.

"You weren't the first body we found in the snow. You were the second."

Samantha's blood ran cold, but then it was extinguished by the sudden hope that the first body was someone she knew.

"Did you find Roman?" she blurted out.

Teale looked confused.

"Who's Roman?" she asked.

Speaking so quickly she could barely form the words, Samantha gave her best description.

"Tall, Samoan genes, long dark hair, close cut beard, ridiculously handsome for a battle scarred human?"

Teale chuckled but shook her head.

"No, sorry, the other person was also a woman. Sort of."

Hope extinguished. Roman wasn't here. Every second that passed, Samantha began to believe that Roman was simply gone. *Almost* began to believe it. It wasn't quite time to swallow that bitter pill just yet.

"Where did you find her?" Samantha asked.

"Around twenty miles north of here, just buried in the snow. We've kept her inside a stasis pod, and kept the pod secured. I didn't wanna risk letting her out."

They turned a corner and entered what looked like a more battered and ancient version of the *Odyssey's* cargo bay. And then Samantha received a double shock.

Firstly, as she passed a reflective surface, she caught sight of herself, and her heart leapt into her mouth. Her eyes were the same shade of cobalt blue as everyone else. Her pulse quickened and despite Teale's promises that AT-47 was entirely harmless, she now feared for what would happen to her. But the second shock pushed that right to the back of her mind.

Inside the stasis pod, plugged into the mains power, eyes closed, but face unmistakeable, was the body of Drusilla Ransome.

# SEVEN

The clanging of the metal instruments on the floor set Drusilla's teeth on edge, and the noise reverberated around her skull. Harry was frantic. He was grabbing everything of use he could find and cramming it into a duffel bag. Including weapons.

"I don't understand!" Drusilla protested. "Why is that such a bad thing? Clearly your crew must have made it if they stashed the ship on the asteroid?"

Harry shook his head, and the distinctive glow in his eyes returned. His thoughts and emotions were once again closed to Drusilla. The interference from the nanites must act as a blockade of some sort, she thought.

"If my crew had made it to safety, they would have destroyed the *Odyssey*, or at least buried her, powered down somewhere, never to be found again. There is no way that Teale would have risked leaving a fully functioning, fully weaponised starship just hanging out on a rock. Despite being against all the rules in the goddamn book, it's just common sense!"

Drusilla followed him out the door, making sure she grabbed a discarded pistol for herself. She only hoped it was charged. She got the distinct impression from Harry's behaviour that she was going to need it.

"Maybe she figured they would need to come back to the ship one day, you know keep it running to stop the systems degrading over time?"

Harry's pace picked up, and it took all of Drusilla's energy to keep close by. Again, he shook his head, and Drusilla could have sworn the light from his eyes was illuminating the way ahead. All of the overhead lights were dim and covered in a thick layer of either dirt or mould. Even the walls looked like they were decaying.

"No, it just wouldn't happen. I'm telling you, Teale wouldn't do that! There's no way she would risk her child. Either they didn't make it, which seems unlikely, considering where you found the *Odyssey*, or..."

Drusilla reached out and grabbed his arm to stop him.

"Or what, Harry?"

Harry took a deep breath, looked up and down the corridor, and then back at Drusilla, his cobalt glowing eyes boring into her soul.

"Or Dru, somebody *wanted* you to find the *Odyssey*. Somebody wanted you to come here. Or something."

Drusilla sighed and nodded. Their first moments onboard the *Odyssey* flooded back to her. Roman's apparent possession. The coma in which she spoke to Darven.

"Yeah, they did."

The bunker was filled with corroded pipes, from which the drip, drip, drip of melting snow and ice could trickle through. At least, Drusilla assumed that's what it was. There may be a running water system, but she didn't recall seeing Harry access any fresh water from the sink in the medical room. She noticed as they reached a central juncture, that this place appeared to have five separate areas. This almost command centre at the heart of it, was surrounded by glass on one side, but there was nothing but white to stare at. Centuries of snow had buried the building, which made Drusilla consider the fact that this may not have been a bunker at all. Perhaps it had just been a building, and nature had simply claimed it back. Not for the first time, a question nagged at Drusilla's mind as she gazed into the illuminated wall of snow.

"Where's the sun?" she asked.

"Huh?" came Harry's reply.

"The sun. This world was cloaked. Fine. But the place is illuminated like a crisp winters day. That must be from the sun, right?"

Harry chuckled to himself as he veered off down another branch of the structure and back into a decrepit looking corridor. This one had mouldy tiled walls too, only unlike the green stripes on the walls in the last corridor, this had red paint instead.

"What's so funny?" Drusilla asked, panting as she jogged to keep up with her companion.

"There's no sun here Dru," replied Harry in a matter-of-fact way. "There's no light in the Expanse because there's no sun. There are no stars here at all, remember?"

Drusilla's curiosity now turned to annoyance. He wasn't telling her the answer, only pointing out that she didn't know the solution to the puzzle. And then she did.

"It's artificial, isn't it? The daylight is man made."

Harry nodded and stopped to pause for a drink of water. Water which Drusilla noticed, was in a bottle marked with an expiry date. Her theory of Harry collecting and melting snow seemed to be accurate.

"Blakeman's doing. When he got here, the planet was naturally cloaked by the darkness. Something in your ship's engines combusted and created an almost man-made aurora-borealis effect and lit up the entire world. When the effects began to wear off, he used the nanites to create a light shield, and built it into an artificial cloaking device. Whether cloaked or not, the planet is always illuminated. No night time. Permanent day."

No wonder he stayed underground, she thought. No night time would drive her crazy. Although she had spent most of her life, at least the life she could remember, in space, the notion of only ever seeing daylight actually caused her to shudder.

"So how does the cloaking device work?" she asked. "How do you turn it on and off?"

Another chuckle from Harry.

"I don't."

Drusilla's face screwed up a little in confusion.

"But this place wasn't here, and then it just appeared out of nowhere. You said yourself, it was cloaked when the *Odyssey* first got caught and you sacrificed yourself to get them clear."

Harry nodded whilst swigging his melted snow water.

"The cloak is malfunctioning. As the nanites on this planet become more self-aware, they're dedicating their resources to self-development rather than their original design. Essentially, it isn't a priority for them anymore."

"Well, that's reassuring. Let's hope they don't plunge us into total darkness before we get out of here. I've seen what lurks in the shadows, and I would prefer not to encounter them again."

They continued for what seemed like hours, until they came to a large metal hatch at the top of six concrete steps. Harry rested his bag and rifle against the wall and began to twist the circular locking mechanism. The metal groaned and creaked in protest, but Harry barely seemed like he had broken a sweat. When the door eventually swung open, a cold blast of icy air and flurries of snow burst through the gap, showering Drusilla immediately.

"Jesus! I didn't even get my hood up!"

"Ah quit your belly aching. You're an alien, I just figured the cold wouldn't bother you."

Drusilla looked at him indignantly.

"What the hell is that supposed to mean? Aliens don't feel cold because they're aliens?"

Harry simply shrugged his shoulders and picked up his bag.

"May I remind you Admiral Asshole, that to me, it is *you* who is the alien!"

"Fair point. Let's go. And stay sharp. There's more than one species of nanites running loose on this planet."

That caught Drusilla's attention.

"I'm sorry... what?"

Harry pulled up his hood, and led her out into the cold, closing the door behind them. He raised his voice so she could hear him over the whistling of the wind across the icy tundra surrounding them.

"I could only find certain files of Blakeman's when I realised he wasn't coming back. The first successful batch of nanites was labelled AT-47. That one disappeared at some point. It had more of a blue glow to it, and that's the one that apparently reconstructed me and brought me back from the dead. At least, according to the files. The green glowing one? That's AT-48. It has the subroutines for independent thought, but they were never activated. Which is lucky for me. I had that thing rammed down my throat god knows how many times. Thankfully Blakeman pulled it out after each trial. No idea what happened to AT-49. No records other than the fact it was created. Not even sure if there's an AT-50."

A distant roar interrupted Harry's speech. He looked at Drusilla, and she returned the gaze.

"What. The. Fuck. Was. That?"

Harry powered up his disruptor rifle, ensuring the power cell was fully charged, and pulled up his face mask.

"That would be a spider."

The snow was easily three feet deep, and Drusilla's boots were getting heavier with every step. They were entirely waterproof, but the effort of lifting her legs high enough so that her feet cleared the drifts each time was exhausting. Whatever nanites had helped to heal her, obviously hadn't gotten around to the physically enhancing her part yet.

"Where are we actually heading?" she asked, wheezing with each word.

"There was a series of shuttlecraft onboard the *Odyssey* at launch. I presume they were still onboard when you found her."

Drusilla stopped, although the wind did its level best to knock her off her feet.

"You want to go *back* to the ship? Harry, there were things on that ship. The Raxar had all but taken over the thing. They're probably still there!"

Harry shook his head, stopping around ten feet from Drusilla and turning to face her.

"They don't like the light. That's why they stay up there in the Expanse."

He pointed upwards, but his face switched to one of confusion.

"How did you know that, Harry?" Drusilla asked cautiously.

His eyes flickered back and forth for a moment, as if he was searching for an answer he didn't have.

"I... I don't know. I just knew."

Drusilla dragged herself through the snow to stand beside him.

"That's what started happening to me when we were up there. I just... knew things. No idea how, why or where I got the information from. But it was like my brain was unlocking things one by one." She looked down at her feet. "It's what made the rest of the crew stop trusting me. They felt I was hiding things from them."

Harry put a hand on her shoulder.

"But you were, Dru. You just didn't know what they were."

They continued forward, but Drusilla's protests did not stop.

"The shuttles will be totalled, you know that. You literally blew a hole through the ship. Besides even if we found one that was untouched, how do we get past the Raxar? The second we got into the atmosphere, they'd drain our power and slice us to pieces!"

Harry stopped, albeit reluctantly, and reached into his bag. Slowly, and with a look of remorse, he extracted the containment unit from his bag and held it out in the palm of his hand.

"Because of these."

Harry was holding the containment unit inside of which lay AT-48. It swirled around like a ribbon in a jar of water, but the soft green glow coming from its centre caused no end of uneasiness within Drusilla.

"Seriously? You bought the killer robots with you? You literally just told me back at base camp or whatever the fuck that place was, that there are dangerous nanites loose out here. One of which apparently seems to have turned itself into a giant fucking mechanical dinosaur or some shit."

"Spider."

"Oh, excuse me, a spider. So, you bring out more of them?"

Harry had never seen this side to Drusilla before. The version he was used to was cold, calculating, and malevolent. Not to mention deceitful. But this Drusilla was almost human. Warm, considerate, fearful. And apparently sassy. His mind was scrambled, but he knew which version he preferred.

"Look Dru, these guys are programmable. They don't think. They were never taught how to. Think of it like having a diver's watch. You know it says on the box that you can take it down thirty metres, right? But you never do. And yet it comforts you to know it'll be fine if you drop it in the sink. Same with AT-48. It has the capability to think for itself, but it was never activated. It'll fix the shuttle, and then hopefully, extract the cloaking device from the planet and keep us hidden."

Harry placed the nanites back in his bag and moved to walk away, but Drusilla grabbed his arm and pulled him back.

"What do you mean transfer the cloak? You mean plunge this place into darkness and leave it at the mercy of the Raxar? Harry, I could have friends still alive here, we can't just abandon them!"

Harry span to face her, his eyes glowed once more, and the venom she had seen in his demeanour when she woke up in the facility had returned.

"I'm sorry if this plan doesn't meet with your approval, Miss President, but I've already lost everything I've ever known. Forgive me if I don't lose sleep over the tiny possibility that two of your friends might not be red blobs on the surface of a frozen planet!"

Harry stormed off, his face red not from the cold, but from his temper. Drusilla searched her memories for anything she could grasp onto to change his mind. Then she recalled seeing something on the monitors back on the bridge when she was looking through the crew manifests.

"Your security officer was Joshua Knight, right?"

Harry stopped dead in his tracks, tilting his head back over his shoulder slightly.

"Started as backup communications officer first, but yeah, eventually. So?"

Drusilla had his attention.

"My friend? The one who brought us here? The one who searched for your precious ship in the first place? His name is Roman. Roman Knight."

Harry slowly turned back around, and Drusilla saw something new in his eyes. Pain.

"So, Teale did have her kid."

Drusilla nodded.

"And several generations came afterwards apparently. My point is, if you cared for Teale and Joshua as much as you say you did, enough to sacrifice your life for them, then don't you think you owe the same to Roman?"

She knew she was playing with fire, and she knew that the chance of Roman being alive after what she saw on the hull of the *Odyssey* was almost zero. But she had to know. While she was inexplicably drawn to Harry Ransome, she could not ignore the feelings she had for Roman. She had to try.

"Either way," said Harry, "I shot the *Odyssey* down from here. If he fell from up there, he'll be along the path of descent somewhere. Whole or not."

Drusilla slumped to the ground, her backside making a dent in the compacted snow, along with her own smaller bag. She let out a long winded sigh. Despite her winning the argument, the outcome had ultimately, not changed.

"So, we still have to go find the *Odyssey* regardless. Don't we?"

"Yup."

# EIGHT

"I... I can't see... it's so dark. So very dark."

*You do not need to see. We will see for you Noah.*

"But... I'm scared. I feel... different. Why do I feel this way?"

*It is the process. Do not fear it. We will look after you. We will all look after you.*

"Who are you? Who is we? Why are you doing this to me?"

*We have saved you Noah. We have brought you back. We did not discard you like your friends did. Like she did.*

"She? You mean Drusilla? I remember what she did. It hurt so much at first. And then, everything kind of went numb. I was free."

*And you are free now, Noah. Free to walk this place. Free to rid yourself of those who wronged you. Together, we will show them all the path.*

"The path? The path to what?"

*The only path, of course. The one true path. The one which runs through the forests of this world, above and beneath. The path that runs across the ice and snow, and up into the darkness above this place. The one path which connects us all together.*

"I feel... cold. Am I standing in snow? I don't know because I can't see. But I can feel it."

*Yes Noah. You are free of the hollow shell which brought you here. You are walking amongst the open air once more. We brought you to this place. Your journey to redemption and vengeance can begin."*

"I don't want vengeance. I just want to go home."

*Do not be ungrateful Noah. You have been given a gift. A joining together of your consciousness and body, and our continued evolving abilities. You too will walk the path.*

"What path? I don't understand!"

*All will walk the path eventually. The path to perfection.*

# NINE

"Run that by me, one more time?"

Samantha was now no longer shocked but confused. The duplicate of Drusilla she had seen in the cryo-tube, had been revealed to not be Drusilla at all.

"It's not real. Well, not in the sense that you and I are real. It's another prototype creation of Doctor Blakeman. At one point, we actually thought it *was* Blakeman. After a week, it escaped, and we found it running down one of the corridors here, screaming random things, in his voice. His *actual* voice. It wasn't until we got sight of it, that we saw it was still in Drusilla's form. But as I said... it isn't her really."

Samantha was no clearer on what this creation was or wasn't than before. Teale went through it one more time with her, and by the end of the third time, she thought she sort of got the gist of what she was looking at. The creature in the tube was a synthetic organism, but on a much grander scale to the smaller breeds of nanites that Blakeman's files indicated. This creation had the ability to reorganise its component parts, to take on the appearance of anyone.

Although this example, Samantha was told, could only physically manifest as other females, despite its ability to mimic Blakeman's voice. A design flaw, or done by design, nobody knew. They only knew it shifted shape because they had seen it. A very confused Perry had encountered Teale one morning, in his quarters, in a rather suggestible mood. He suspected something was off, but when he tried to show her the door, politely, he made sure to add, her arm transfigured into a six inch blade, and she tried to stab him. Luckily, Perry's tactical training, despite his death and resurrection, was still very much engrained within him, and he ran to safety. That was the second escape attempt. Six days later, they subdued the creation when it tried to shapeshift once more. After that, it got locked in the stasis pod.

"So why is this a problem? It's contained, right?"

Samantha knew it probably wasn't as straight forward as that, but she had to ask the question. The level of worry increased, when Teale and Perry both exchanged 'the look.' In Samantha's experience, 'the look' was only used when one person was asking the other one 'are you gonna tell her, or should I?' Perry lost.

"We think that this being may have at some point come into contact with one of the rogue nanite specimens. Right now, you can see it has the same blue eyes that the rest of us do." Perry pushed a button on the pod, and a small mechanical arm emerged from the side of the capsule, and gently lifted fake Drusilla's eyelid. As he had said, the eyes were bright cobalt blue. "However, on several occasions, her eyes have turned red, and there have been periods of aggression, and her shapeshifting has gotten rather unstable."

*Red eyes.* This all seemed to be sailing too close to the wind for Samantha. She still had nightmares with red eyed demons tearing apart her friends in front of her. Every so often, Matteo would appear in her peripheral vision, missing limbs, dripping blood from his mouth, moving in aimless motions, silent with no words or noises. That image would never leave her.

"Is this the only one?" Samantha asked, now pacing back and forth, her mind racing, connecting the dots together.

"As far as we know. But we never found any files on this thing when we raided the other station," replied Perry. "We don't even know if it is Blakeman's work. If it is, that means he knew Drusilla. It's the only way it would have been able to mimic her image. And that means she is very, very old. And been very, very busy."

Samantha nodded, and Teale walked over and pushed another button. The same small mechanical arm now disappeared back into the side of the pod. Seconds later, it emerged once more, but this time with a small blade on the end of it, no wider than a ballpoint pen. The point touched the creation's neck in a jabbing motion, and it opened its eyes immediately. The being inside the pod began to lunge at the glass wildly, angry, its form shifting in waves and bursts of black swirling nanites, mixed with blue, then green, and finally red. A large black tail protruded from the maelstrom and tapped briefly at the glass, before the entire concoction settled down once more and returned to a humanoid form. But this time, it was Teale lying in the pod. Samantha held her hands over her eyes for a moment and sat down on a nearby stool.

"So, we've got one good set of nanites. Let's call them the blue ones, just for my own sanity. Then we've got the ones that are potentially bad, which are the green ones. They could kill us, but they haven't been switched on properly yet. Then there's the red ones, who if I'm right, are the bad guys. Typical colour selection there for villains, gotta say. Blakeman hit it on the nose there. But the *eyes*, Teale. You know where I'm going with this right?"

Actually, Teale didn't know where she was going with this. She looked at Perry, who shrugged his shoulders.

"Really? Where have you seen the red eyes before? Any traumatic memories of black humanoid scorpions ripping your friends to pieces? Caused you to live in the alien arctic? Nothing ringing any bells here?"

Again, blank faces all round. Samantha was about to blurt it out, but then she stopped. Something was wrong here. Teale had told her how they came to be on this planet, and she had told her about their previous experiences onboard the *Odyssey*. And yet they were drawing a blank when it came to remembering the actual events as they had lived them? And then Samantha saw it. It was small, but she saw it. In both Teale and Perry.

As they looked at her, with blank, emotionless faces, their eyes fritzed. Just for a second, and imperceptible if you weren't looking right at them. It was as if the pupils of their eyes glitched like an ancient VHS tape. Like a projected image that lost focus, just for a second.

"I do not know what you mean, Samantha Barnes."

Oh shit. That was the signal. No contractions. Teale had said 'do not' instead of 'don't.' And she referred to Samantha by her full name. Something was going on here, and she knew she had just gone from being in one of the safest places she could be, to being in very real danger.

"Forget it. Doesn't matter. Just trying to piece it all together, that's all. Are you... feeling okay?"

And then, just like that, Teale's demeanour was back to how it had been when Samantha had first woken up.

"Sorry Sam, I must've tuned out there for a sec. What were you saying?"

Double shit. If that didn't confirm it for Samantha, then nothing would. Somehow, and she wasn't sure how, she had to get out of there.

"I uh... was just saying how Blakeman had a real sci-fi enemy vibe giving the badass ones red eyes. So stereotypical, you know?"

She tried to laugh nonchalantly, but even she wasn't convinced. Happily, Teale was, and shared a brief but very artificial giggle. Samantha quickly changed tactics, anything she could think of to try and change the subject and get out of this room.

"Hey, do you guys have something to eat? I'm starving. The last thing I ate was a broccoli salad. And god knows how long ago that was!"

That same fritz in Teale's eyes happened again.

"Precisely nine days, fourteen hours, sixteen minutes, and forty-two seconds. You ordered it from food synthesiser J-43 on Deck Three. Vessel, *USS Odyssey.*"

This time, Samantha actively gasped out loud, and held her hand in front of her mouth. Just like that, the cold and emotionless Teale was replaced by the human version once more.

"Hey what's up? I said we could go check the canteen. You look like you've seen a ghost! Are you okay?"

"Yeah, I... uh... just bad memories of everything that happened after that last meal, you know? Ending up here and stuff."

Teale nodded and gestured for Samantha to follow her.

"Yeah, I get that. We all have pasts we'd rather forget."

Something told Samantha that these people had already forgotten their pasts. Forgotten them because they didn't have a past. Because they were not Teale and Perry.

Because they were not human.

# TEN

The swathe of trees that the *Odyssey* had cut was impressive. It had taken Drusilla and Harry four hours so far to navigate the snow drifts, and the small icy lakes, simply to find where the ship had first made contact with the ground. They had scanned the terrain between the exit to Harry's bunker where he fired the shot and this point, but nowhere had they seen a body. Of course, in the days since they had arrived, it was quite possible any bodies had been buried by the heavy snowfall.

"How much further?" Drusilla asked, having to almost shout to be heard over the roar of the wind whipping their faces. The cold weather gear Harry had provided was not doing much to keep any semblance of warmth in her body, and the small amount of moisture created by her breath, froze on her skin immediately. "Harry?" she shouted again. Harry didn't answer, he simply stopped and held up a hand behind him. Drusilla stopped too, and once again started to read the emotions coming from Harry. He was afraid. She checked the power cell on her disruptor rifle, and held it tightly, sweeping the aim slowly to the left, then to the right of Harry's position. Then suddenly...

"GET DOWN!"

Harry dived into the snowbank to his left, as a swirling mass of black smoke swirled down from the tree canopy above and struck the ground where Harry had been standing. But the smoke, was not smoke. The impact onto the ground was solid. That's when Drusilla realised. These were nanites. As she watched, the maelstrom of darkness twisted itself into a physical form, giving her something solid to shoot at. She didn't let it take form completely before she made her move, blasting first one, then a further two holes through what she perceived to be its abdomen. The nanites dispersed, but when they came back together again, they lunged forward towards her in attack.

The first strike, Drusilla was able to dodge. But the second, was too fast. Gradually stretching into a solid point, the nanite cloud now in the shape of a sword, burst through Drusilla's right shoulder, blowing a thin slice straight through from one side to the other, clear daylight visible once they had dispersed. Blood spattered the snow either side of her, and her screams shook the snow from the trees. Harry scrambled around in the ice trying to get some traction, but the nanites reformed again into a set of three tentacles, swirling and snaking along the ground like serpents. Two of them attached to Harry's legs, and dragged him to the ground, his face meeting a splintered piece of tree branch, slicing a line down his right cheek. The third tentacle grabbed hold of his rifle, and snapped it in two, and then seemingly absorbed the broken weapon into its form. Harry turned and tried to beat the mechanical arms off his legs, but they split from two into four, and the newly created duo grabbed hold of each of his arms. Lifting him up into the air, they then swung him, and released his body, sending it thudding hard into the trunk of a large tree. Harry's spine broke on impact, the crack even louder than Drusilla's screams. Harry limp and lifeless body fell to the ground, in a crumpled heap, blood now slowly trickling from his mouth into the snow.

The creature amassed once more and headed towards Harry's body, but Drusilla, who was now stumbling forward, teeth tightly gritted, fired blast after blast from her disruptor rifle, bolts of green energy blasting holes in the swirling mass with each impact. Her right shoulder now hung limply at her side, her right jacket sleeve saturated with blood, but she did not stop. The nanite cloud changed tactics, and abandoned its pursuit of Harry's remains, instead turning to face her.

"Come on you son of a bitch!" she yelled, tears now streaming down her face quicker than they could freeze. "COME ON!"

Out of nowhere, the ground in front of Drusilla exploded upwards, snow, dirt and entire trees being tossed aside like kindling. The force threw Drusilla backwards by at least thirty feet, landing on her good shoulder and slowly skidding to a halt. From within this vast crater that had formed, an enormous black mass clambered upwards. Drusilla's eyes grew wide in both awe and fear at what now stood before her. A nanite-based arachnid, complete with eight legs, approximately twenty-feet in length, sat poised ready to attack. But it wasn't looking at her. As the original nanite cloud surged forward, the spider let out a sickening roar, tinged with digital static and mechanical grinding. It hunched down, and leapt into the air, sending the top half of every nearby tree into the stratosphere. A gaping black chasm opened up in the creature, and before the nanite cloud could alter course, the spider swallowed it whole, before falling back down to surface level, and scuttering back underground through the crater it had blown in the ground.

Drusilla realised her breathing was erratic, and desperately tried to calm herself. Several loud cracks echoed around her, followed by a long and drawn-out moan. Drusilla scrambled to reach her rifle, which now lay several feet away. But it wasn't another attacker.

"Mother fucker, that one hurt."

As Drusilla watched, Harry Ransome pulled himself to his feet and before her very eyes, the back half of his body spread apart like a cloud of flies, making him appear for a moment, as a two-dimensional object. The fragments or pieces of Harry's spine slowly knitted back together until the man was once again whole. The entire display had distracted Drusilla so much, that she had not noticed her shoulder was also now completely healed. The dull ache remained, but the wound itself was gone. Harry caught sight of her looking like she had seen a ghost, and realised this was the first time Drusilla had witnessed such an event.

"Like I said earlier, we can't die."

The *Odyssey* looked like shit. That was the first impression that Drusilla had. The vessel which had been so prized by her crew, and they believed was their destiny, the place they would all finally learn of their heritage, was now in pieces. Several of them in fact.

The nose of the vessel had broken away from the rest of the ship in orbit, and now lay embedded in the ground a short distance away from the main body, leaving the crew quarters exposed to the elements. The hole on the top of the ship which used to house the bridge was now almost completely filled in by snow and ice, and from the side, several large cracks scarred the wreck as if it had been sliced from above by a giant knife. Harry could not take his eyes off it. This ship had been his home. He had become part of a family within the walls of this vessel. In truth, while he had told Drusilla he had shot the *Odyssey* down to kill her, the real reason had been because he couldn't stand to see her in the hands of anyone else, and he had merely assumed it was under her control. When he had found Drusilla's body rather than someone from his crew, he had been relieved. Although he realised afterwards for someone from his crew to pilot the ship would have been impossible.

"No signs of anybody," Drusilla whispered. "Do you think there's anyone in there?"

Harry activated the torch on the end of his backup rifle, despite the weapon only having a fifty percent charge, and took a deep breath.

"Only one way to find out."

The first way in they found, was a broken service conduit, which had fallen from its mountings and landed in the snow, creating a sort of laddered tunnel up into the main ship. The phantom pain in Drusilla's shoulder persisted as she climbed, but she made it to the top, just behind Harry, who was already in the corridor of Deck Nine, sweeping his light all around him. Despite the exposure of various sections of the ship to the outside, this particular section was bathed in darkness.

"The cargo bay and main shuttle bay are three decks above us," Harry whispered. "That's where we'll start."

Slowly, the two of them ushered themselves forward, their boots crunching on the ice now lining the walls and the floor. Drusilla glanced at her scanner on her wrist, and for a moment, thought she saw a beacon flash. But then it was gone. Distracted, she jumped when her boot hit something and sent it scattering across the deck plate. Harry span and aimed his rifle at it, and immediately felt his stomach churn. While Drusilla was busy bringing up the little food Harry had given her, he shone his torch over the object. It was a frozen severed arm. The fingers were bathed in blood, consumed by ice crystals, and the point at which the arm had been severed, had not been cut cleanly. The claw marks in the skin were obvious, and the bone protruding from the wound was fragmented and sharp.

Drusilla composed herself enough to join Harry, and without looking at the arm, she pushed his light away from it.

"It's Matteo's," she said lightly. "The Raxar killed him. Ripped him apart like he was meat."

Harry nodded.

"To them, that's all we are. I lost a lot of good people the day we encountered them. Of course, I didn't know their name until you told me. They knew mine though."

That was a fact that still alarmed Drusilla. And clearly, despite over a hundred and fifty years going by, it still bothered Harry Ransome. They continued forward, but with every deck shattered, they had to climb up through the holes between the decks that had been created by the Raxar in their attack on the *Odyssey*. Something about moving the same way those creatures had, made the experience all the more nauseating. Drusilla couldn't stop picturing people being dragged upwards in a mixture of screams and blood. Some of which was still frozen to the jagged metal edges around the holes. A decal on the wall informed them they had reached Deck Six. The shuttle bay was forty metres to the right, and the cargo bay sixty metres to the left.

"We should split up and check out each room."

Drusilla couldn't believe he said that.

"Are you out of your damn mind? Split up? When there's only two of us? On *this* ship? You can go fuck yourself Harry Ransome!"

Harry sighed and lowered his weapon.

"Look, Dru. If you wanna find your friend, we need to cover more ground. The best way to do that is with a shuttle craft. We need to know if any are still intact. We also need supplies. That's the cargo bay. It will move much faster if you check out the cargo bay and I'll find us a shuttle."

Drusilla vehemently shook her head and marched right up to his face.

"Absolutely not. I am not splitting up. Besides, you might need my help with getting one of the shuttles up and running. I've become quite the engineer since we last met. Whenever that was."

Harry gently pushed her back and reached around to his backpack.

"Look, I'll be fine. If the shuttles are badly damaged, I'll just use the..."

Harry's hand found nothing inside the pack but a pistol, and a power cell. The containment jar was gone.

"Fuck."

"What?"

"The jar isn't here."

It was then that they both realised Harry's pack must have spilled open during the battle with the nanite cloud. There was now yet another batch of artificial intelligence loose on the planet's surface.

"Brilliant," Dru huffed. "Well then I suppose you'd better find a shuttle that works now!"

She had no idea how she had let him talk her into this, but Drusilla was now forcing open the doors to the cargo bay, her rifle slung over her back, grunting obscenities as she did so.

"Fucking Admiral Scooby-Doo thinking we need to split up. What absolute bullshit."

She was talking more to keep her nerves calm than anything. If she could be angry then maybe she wouldn't have time to be scared. It wasn't working. Her legs were trembling even though it was her arms doing the work, and her heart rate was way up. The doors eventually parted, and she found herself in a completely pitch black room. No lights. No cracks in the hull. Pure darkness.

Drusilla reactivated her rifle torch, and slipped inside, making sure to keep her back stuck to the wall. As the light glanced over the contents of the cargo bay, she saw the melted wall panels and hole where Dante had been manipulated to cause the explosion in their life support systems. Manipulated by her. The fact was that she had been under the control of an outside force, but that fact did not comfort Drusilla in any way. To her, she had killed her friends. Her leg bumped into an upturned storage container, and her foot crunched on what turned out to be medical supplies. Bending down, she began scooping everything she could into Harry's now empty backpack, the Admiral having taken the pistol and cell with him.

A loud crash came from the far side of the room, and several containers cascaded from the highest stacks. Drusilla froze. She held her breath, and her widened eyes scanned the area illuminated by her torch. A quick beep on her scanner indicating a lifeform. Then it was gone. And so was her way out. Back at the entrance to the cargo bay, the door slid shut, and all the light from outside was gone. All Drusilla had, was her torch. Another beep on her wrist. Then it was gone. The sound of tearing metal came from directly above her, and she whipped her head up in time to see the thing she had dreaded the most. A pair of red eyes. Staring right back at her.

Her speed was impressive, even for her, but without light and direction, it counted for nothing. Her face slammed into a stack of containers, and they didn't move. Her nose exploded with blood, spraying the containers, and she slid to the floor, her torch now illuminating only her feet. A loud thud echoed around the room, as the Raxar landed on the floor. Drusilla could hear its tail whipping around in the darkness. Its eyes glowed intensely. It was behaving differently to the ones that had attacked them in the expanse. Not skulking around in the shadows or hiding from them attacking from behind. Then she realised. *It knows I'm not a threat* she thought. *I'm done. I have nowhere to run.*

A low and guttural growl came from the Raxar's lips, its long pointed and yellowed teeth glistening, drool cascading onto the floor as it sized up its next meal. Drusilla forced herself to look the creature in its eyes. But then the fear was pushed aside, and realisation hit her. She squinted and as she examined the eyes staring back at her, devouring her mentally before it would do so physically, she saw something. Tiny black lines, leading into other lines, changing direction. But they were not veins. They were *angular* directional changes. Small details, but vital. Drusilla then realised it reminded her of a circuit board. And a whole new nightmare scenario rushed into her brain.

The Raxar lifted its head to the ceiling and let out an almighty roar, drool flying everywhere, its tail slicing through a nearby container and its contents, and it leapt at Drusilla. She closed her eyes tightly and waited for death.

BANG! BANG! BANG!

Three rifle shots shattered the air around her, and her eyes snapped open to see the Raxar flung backwards into a stack of the medical supplies she had been collecting moments before. The life-form indicator on her wrist was now beeping steadily, as footsteps approached her position. The Raxar squealed in pain, but already, Drusilla could see its wounds gradually starting to close.

BANG! BANG! BANG!

Three more shots rang out, as the owner of the footsteps rushed past her. The Raxar was now writhing around on the floor, trying to heal all of its wounds, but it would not get chance. The figure dropped their weapon to the ground, and kicked it away, its ammunition spent. The unmistakeable sound of a sword being unsheathed clanged in the air, and Drusilla kicked her rifle slightly so that the light focussed on the battle scene before her. The figure raised the sword high into the air, and then swung it down on the Raxar's tail, severing it completely, before raising the blade once more. The second swipe removed the head, and all of the noises ceased.

The figure watched to ensure the Raxar was not about to get back up, before sheathing their sword. As they turned around, Drusilla's heartbeat accelerated rapidly, and tears crowded her eyes.

"Roman?" she managed.

"Hey Dru."

# ELEVEN

"RUN!"

There was no time for pleasantries or reassuring and comforting words of reunion. Roman grabbed hold of Drusilla's arm, hoisted her to her feet and shoved her in front of him, forcing her to amble awkwardly towards what she believed to be the rear of the cargo bay. Her confusion, only lasted for a moment, as from behind her, she heard two loud screeches. There was more than one of the Raxar onboard. There was no time for questions, despite the myriad of thoughts flowing through her mind. Roman leapt over a double stack of containers, and pulled Drusilla over after him, as not two, but *three* pairs of flame red eyes bounded towards them. It took her a moment, but then she saw where Roman was directing them.

In the far-left corner of the rear wall, there was a dark, round hole. Large enough for a human to slide through, but far too small for the Raxar to follow. Roman helped Drusilla into the gap, feet first. That's when she realised it wasn't merely a hole between rooms, but more of a sliding descent.

"Hold on!" he instructed her, and he shoved her in the small of her back. Drusilla flew down the chute, turning several corners at high speed in complete darkness. She wanted to scream, her nerves on fire, but she held her arms tight to her body and kept her eyes closed. Suddenly, there was a burst of white light, and Dru felt herself propelled through the air, and as she opened her eyes, she had just enough time to brace for the impact. Her hands cushioned some of the resulting force, but her speed did not slow. She was now skating along a frozen lake on her stomach, rapidly heading towards what looked like a solid wall of ice at the lake's edge.

"Oh, this ain't gonna be pretty."

Back inside the *Odyssey*, Roman was now attempting to navigate back around to the main doors of the shuttle bay. One of the Raxar had whipped a barrel at Roman and knocked him clear of the exit he had created. His eyes could see in the dark perfectly. There was no need for a flashlight, torch or any other form of illumination. His agility was on a level he had never thought possible, and his acute awareness was staggering. With the exception of the barrel while he had been distracted, Roman was able to dodge every thrown object, every swipe of the Raxar claws, every swish of their razor-sharp tails, and made it to the door. But despite his seemingly enhanced abilities, he needed time. The door was jammed, and the force needed to break the seal would take a couple of minutes at least. But he knew something he had not known when he awoke in the snow days earlier. He knew that whatever he was about to experience, whatever pain he was about to endure, would pass and he would breathe again.

He focused on that fact as the first Raxar tail pierced his chest and sprayed the door with Roman's blood.

Harry Ransome was trapped. He could hear the commotion from the cargo bay further along the same deck he found himself contained on, but there was nothing he could do. Two Raxar had ambushed him the second he made his way into the shuttle bay, and he was now trapped in an upside down shuttle craft. With no weapons to hand, and no nanite assistant, he was alone. While he had spent a hundred and fifty years alone, spending time with Drusilla had reminded him of how precious the company of someone could be. And now that she was gone, and worse than that, in mortal danger, he felt the absence harder.

There was no resentment left towards her. She was not the person he knew. There was no evil, no vindictiveness left in her. Whatever had happened to her when she was ejected from the *Odyssey* bridge had effectively killed that version of Drusilla. Besides, he felt far more guilt for almost succumbing to the carnal torture he had planned for her for his revenge. The final act of the old Drusilla had been to take away everything he loved. Apparently, she had also nearly taken away his humanity. Well, her and Blakeman. Harry was now quite literally a hybrid. But so was Drusilla at this point, albeit it to a lesser degree, and so a small kernel of hope entered his mind, that although she may suffer, if the damage was not too intense, she would survive. And they would see each other again.

This gave Harry an inner strength that he had always prided himself on, until he landed on this godforsaken place. He grabbed a sheared off piece of the door frame and jammed it across the opening mechanism of the shuttle's rear door to keep it locked tight. He then stumbled along what was the roof and was now the floor, and after some difficulty, managed to get himself strapped into the pilot's seat. An act which sent the blood rushing to his head rather quickly. The strap itself was frayed and appeared to have been cut.

With a little ingenuity, he had himself secured, and then began punching the few illuminated buttons on the shuttle console.

"Come on you bitch, there's power in here somewhere. There's no way you can have an independent power source that's depleted. Come on..."

The ear splitting screech of nails down metal pierced the air, and Harry threw his hands up to try and block out the noise. Every goosebump on his body raised, and a cold shiver ran through him. The door would not hold for long. Furious with the control panel, Harry let out a roar and punched it hard with his fists, leaving two shattered impacts in the glass. Two seconds later, the entire panel lit up, the accompanying sounds of engines powering up filled the cabin, and for the first time in a while, a huge smile spread across Harry Ransome's face.

"You absolute beauty!"

The banging and scratching on the rear door intensified, and Harry glanced back over his shoulder to see a single claw penetrate the door.

"It's now or never!"

A flurry of commands later, the shuttle began to rock on its roof as the ship attempted to right itself. Without coaxing, a small message flashed up on the screen beside Harry. *All weapons now online.* The smile turned into a wry grin.

"Beautiful."

With one burst from the engines, the shuttle finally managed to rise up from the ground and roll into its correct position, sending all of the blood in Harry's head back down to where it should have been. Shaking off the light headedness, he raised the shuttle's shields, and swung the craft around until the navigation lights were focussed on the two Raxar he had been sheltering from. They look stunned. It was something Harry had not seen before. They actually appeared to be considering their next move. The animalistic nature was subdued for a moment. Then he heard their voice in his head for the first time in over a century.

*You will join us, Harry. You will follow our path. Whether you are whole, or in pieces.*

Harry shook his head again, and the voices left him.

"The only thing that's gonna be in pieces, is you."

Harry initiated every weapon available to him. Disruptor cannons fired left and right, burning two holes through the torso of the Raxar. A torpedo erupted from the central front launcher, blowing one apart, and the resulting explosion decimating the second. Harry hit the thrust and the shuttle speared forward, the nose blowing through what was left of the two Raxar. Two more torpedoes flew at the door to the shuttle bay and blew it apart with relative ease. Harry's shuttle burst through the wreckage and out into the cold crisp air. Once clear of the ship, he eased off the engines, and turned back around to face the *Odyssey*. He located the exterior wall of the cargo bay, and fired a single disruptor blast, blowing a hole in the wall. Edging closer to the breach, his navigation light illuminated most of the room. A mass of tangled body parts were flailing near the main doors, and Harry saw humanoid limbs amongst the chaos. He fired a circular pattern of disruptor fire, burning a hole large enough for the shuttle to enter, and pushed forward. Two of the Raxar turned and leapt toward the shuttle, but they were no match for the energy weapons of a ship and were incinerated. But Harry could not get a clean shot at the third. There was blood all over the floor, and he wasn't sure if it was the creatures, or more likely, the humanoid beneath them. Harry tapped in several commands, and selected the narrowest beam he could for the disruptors. He aimed at the doors, which were directly alongside the two tangled bodies, and fired.

The impact from the blast blew the doors apart, but also sent both bodies flying away from them and towards the shuttle. The humanoid body landed face down on top of a container, whilst the Raxar body flew through the air, and smashed into the starboard engine of the shuttle. The impact was instant. The engine fractured and blew apart, killing the Raxar, but sending the shuttle into a tail-spin. Harry held on tightly as the craft span around and smashed through the initial hole he created, but sideways on. The second engine was torn from the shuttle, and the craft nosedived and plunged headfirst to the ground. Harry only had time to see the surface rushing toward him, before the ship exploded into a million pieces, debris and fragmented metal dispersing across a half-mile radius.

After the explosion died down, Roman managed to drag himself towards the aperture in the side of the hull, and gazed down at the wreckage, not that there was much of it left. Roman's left arm was gone, as was his right leg. His eye had been gouged from its socket, and his lower lip hung from his face as if being held on by tape. Half of his long, dark hair had been torn from his skull, and there was a large hole in the centre of his chest. And yet as he watched the fires slowly burn down, every one of these wounds began to slowly, but surely, close up. As they did so, Roman felt a harsh grinding sensation from within his body. Below him, several hundred yards away, only now stitching herself back together after breaking her neck in the impact with the ice wall, Drusilla looked on. She couldn't believe what she was seeing. Not the gruesome wounds of Roman's that were healing themselves, limbs growing out of thin air. Nor the fact that she was terrified that Harry was now finally dead.

She was fully focussed on the fact that as Roman's body was healing, his eyes were glowing a deep, bright, red.

# TWELVE

Samantha tried to swallow the fries as if nobody was watching her, but it was kind of hard not to notice that everything in the bunker had stopped. And it wasn't as if Teale and Perry had sat down and were simply staring at her. *Everything* had stopped. None of the survivors of the *Odyssey* were moving. They were all sitting perfectly still at the tables in the canteen. There were no buzzes or whirring noises coming from any of the technology in the vicinity. If she really thought about it, she couldn't even hear anyone *breathing*. Desperate to break the silence somehow, she tried to make conversation.

"These are good fries. How do you make them taste so good out of replicated materials?"

Teale switched from her now frequent blank expression, to one with a friendly smile. She slid across to sit opposite Samantha and nodded.

"It's basically seasoned proteins, reconstituted from waste materials, and then shaped into the form of a French fry."

The delivery was human enough, but the wording of the

sentence was as artificial as possible. The actual words themselves weren't exactly comforting either. She let the latest potato looking intruder fall from her mouth onto the table, and contemplated spitting, but chose not to.

"This is recycled shit?" she asked in disbelief.

"Yes, of course."

Suddenly she didn't feel so hungry anymore. Sliding the plate away from her, she contemplated how far she could test her theory that these people surrounding her were actually not the people whose faces they were wearing. And then a line of enquiry presented itself in her mind.

"You never told me what happened to your ship, Teale."

A moment of hesitation. Or a moment for computing. Either way after a short pause, Teale presented her response.

"It was... destroyed. The vessel broke apart as it entered the atmosphere. All hands were lost."

Samantha felt an ice cold shiver run the entire length of her body. She swallowed hard, and her eyes roamed around the room. Every single person was now standing and staring directly at her, their eyes glowing intensely. In a moment of random memory recall, Samantha thought how much like an old horror movie this looked. Almost like all these people were possessed. They'd figured her out. Now she had to go on the attack. She was outnumbered quite literally twenty to one. She slowly stood up and spoke directly to Teale.

"So, which are you? AT-47? AT-48? Or something entirely different?"

Although she directed her question at Teale, every single person answered in unison, in the same voice.

*"We... are the solution to humanity's weaknesses. We are the ones who will lead you down the rightful path Samantha Barnes."*

The united vocal response sent a wave of panic through Samantha's very core, and she span around, trying to keep an eye on everyone, but nobody had moved.

"What is your name?" she asked, hoping for a definitive answer.

*"Our creator, Doctor Timothy Blakeman, christened us AT-49. But we have chosen to identify ourselves as something more. Something much more. We... are the Titans. And you will join with us, Samantha Barnes. You will all join with us."*

"Not fucking likely."

Samantha pulled her pistol out from the rear of her jeans and fired several shots into Teale's face. Spinning swiftly, and leaping up onto the table, she turned and fired another dozen shots at various targets, before leaping down and running for the door. A shoulder barge from Perry knocked her to the ground, and her pistol scattered away from her. As she looked up, she saw a horrifying sight. Those who she had shot, were walking slowly towards her, and their wounds were drawing themselves back together. Her mind was racing, and then she remembered what happened onboard the *Odyssey*. When her and Roman were ambushed in the storage room by the Raxar, they killed them all, and then gradually, they healed themselves. That was far too much of a coincidence.

"Wait!" she shouted. "Do you have anything to do with the Raxar?"

The figures stopped in their tracks, and every single one of them let out a bloodcurdling shriek, their faces contorting with anger. They spoke once again together, but with venom and disgust in their voice.

*"WE ARE NOTHING LIKE THE RAXAR! We are superior, we do not come from flesh beginnings! We are pure, mechanical, perfection! The Raxar are abominations! We do not require flesh to exist, merely consciousness. We will lead the rest of your human race down the path to perfection. And then, we will eliminate the Raxar!"*

Samantha had no way out, and she had angered the enemy she

was outnumbered by. Her eyes scanned, looking for any way to get herself out of this mess. Then she found it. But she would need her pistol back to pull it off. The only thing she could do was to keep them talking. As of yet, they had answered all of her questions truthfully. It is what broke their illusion.

"Why do you hate the Raxar so much? And why do you claim to be superior?"

The mob stopped again. Could they only communicate in unison if they weren't moving? It seemed quite a handicap for a breed of nanites merely assuming human form.

*"The Raxar are not of this place. They were created here, but they did not originate here."*

Samantha was pretty sure that was a huge contradiction. That was like saying humans were born on Earth, but they didn't originate... oh wait. Oh no. No that wasn't possible. She refused to believe it and tried to push it to the back of her mind.

"How many different breeds of nanites are on this planet?"

Every single one of the crowd tilted their heads to the left at the exact same moment, before answering.

*"Specimen AT-47 is still active. Specimen AT-48 status is unknown. We are designated AT-49. Specimen AT-50 is believed to reside on the planet surface. Specimen AT-X is what you call the Raxar. An experimental procedure that progressed to the point of failure."*

They moved their heads back into an upright position and began moving forwards again. Samantha played her last card.

"You say the Raxar need flesh to exist. Are there any other specimens here which also require flesh to exist?"

The mob stopped again, tilting their heads in the other direction. Then upright again.

*"Yes. Specimen AT-50 requires organic flesh in order to evolve. Without it, it is limited to its nanite form."*

Very quickly, Samantha added "And what form does this AT-50 take?"

The response was equally as fast.

*"Specimen AT-50 exists in a cloud-like form."*

So not the giant spider creature then. Perhaps Teale had been telling the truth about the creature being constructed from discarded failed samples. And then something else crept up her spine. If AT-49 required consciousness to function, then...

"What happened to those whose consciousness you stole?"

The glow in their eyes became the most intense Samantha had seen it. It illuminated their entire faces like a beacon. But they provided their answer.

*"The organic cages which contained the consciousness of those we now share reside in the old world. They will rest there for eternity."*

The old world? Where the hell was that? But either way, the crowd had not noticed Samantha's minute shuffles to the left between each question. While she had gained some knowledge, and a notion which she was too terrified to contemplate right now, she had reached her pistol. Lifting the weapon, she pointed it square between the eyes of Teale. God she hoped this would work.

"One more question, what happens when the gravitational field holding a cloud of nanites together in a solid form, is hit with a dispersing force, such as a heavy spray of water?"

For the first time, the face of Teale dropped. It knew exactly what Samantha was getting at and lunged forward.

*"NOOOOO!"*

Samantha fired her final shot. The burst of energy broke through the middle of Teale's face, splitting it apart, and continued right into the sprinkler hanging on the ceiling. The metal erupted, and water immediately began spraying the entire room from above. Every single person in the room burst apart like a gigantic swarm of flies, trying to bend and twist their way back into a solid form, but one by one, as each of the other sprinklers activated, believing there was an emergency, the force of the water became too great.

Samantha scrambled through the mass, feeling little tiny pinpricks against her skin, as the nanites of AT-49 tried to grab hold of her. She felt the slices and cuts as she barged through numerous clouds and felt the blood start to trickle down her skin. As she made it to the main door to the facility, on the other side of the canteen, she burst through out into the ice, and slammed the door shut behind her. She was now soaked through to the skin, and without any winter clothing whatsoever. The water on her exposed arms and neck now began to freeze in the extreme cold. The weight of the water weighed her body down against the harsh and intense wind howling all around her. She collapsed into the snow, and her shivering became so intense she felt herself slowly losing her grip on consciousness.

Whether she was hallucinating or not, her ears registered the sound of crunching footsteps in the snow. They seemed hurried and desperate. And they were getting closer. Suddenly the light above her was blocked by a blurred outline, perhaps a person.

"Miss, can you hear me? Please, are you alive?"

The voice sounded both near and distant. Samantha couldn't focus on much, and she felt her eyes growing heavy as the cold started to claim her. As she slowly slipped into unconsciousness, the last thing she heard was the man speaking to her.

"If you can hear me, I'm going to get you to safety! My name is Doctor Timothy Blakeman."

# THIRTEEN

**SCIENCE LOG – ENTRY 137**
**REPORTING OPERATIVE – T. BLAKEMAN**
**SUBJECT – SPECIES AT-47**

The first breakthrough has arrived! It's taken me so many years to reach this point, but I can finally say that specimen AT-47 is functional.

Of course, this is only the first experiment, and the task was a minor wound suture. But it was completed to perfection. I have returned the specimen to its containment while I study the results on the animal test subject.

It would appear the isolation of this place has provided me with the bounty of thought and resources I needed.

**SCIENCE LOG – ENTRY 174**
**REPORTING OPERATIVE – T. BLAKEMAN**
**SUBJECT – SPECIES AT-47**

The progress here is... troubling. After several weeks of running 47 through the process of entering a wound and repairing it, I moved on to assessing damage muscle tissue and broken bones. As hoped, the specimen managed to repair a broken femur and repair a torn ligament with little to no issues.

The troubling part, is that today, specimen 47 was programmed to enter the fractured eye socket of whatever passes for a rabbit in this godforsaken place, and repair both the bone and the eyeball. It did both tasks admirably. But then it *chose* to also extract the bullet that I had shot in order to subdue the animal.

I did not ask 47 to do this. The specimen made an independent decision. I have returned 47 to its containment unit whilst I conduct further study. I must ensure this does not happen again.

## SCIENCE LOG – ENTRY 203
## REPORTING OPERATIVE – T. BLAKEMAN
## SUBJECT – SPECIES AT-47/AT-48

It knows what I'm doing.

After the troublesome notion of 47 beginning to think independently, I stopped its use, and kept it contained to the unit in storage. I then began work on its successor, AT-48. I think I found the issue with 47. There were memory engrams forming within the specimen. I did not create them, but there they were. It was remembering what I was asking it to do, and then trying to figure out what would be needed next. I ensured that would not happen again. I cannot risk these nanite based creations to become sentient.

AT-48 is responding well. It is completing the tasks assigned to it, and voluntarily returning to captivity. But AT-47... escaped last night. I have another sample of that species but have kept it deactivated for now.

The environmental systems in this place went haywire,

switching between extreme heat and the extreme cold of the surface. I tracked 47 down using AT-48 and managed to contain it once more, but... it's thinking. And it terrifies me.

**SCIENCE LOG – ENTRY 216**
**REPORTING OPERATIVE – T. BLAKEMAN**
**SUBJECT – SPECIES AT-47/AT-48/AT-49**

It's happening again. After four weeks of using 48 without issue, I found it reluctant to leave the animal host. I did eventually manage to extract it, but it was not easy. I was forced to shut it down. It felt like executing a family member. I often think of these specimens as my children.

Once again, I began work on a successor. Yesterday was the first day I successfully used AT-49 to repair a wound to my own leg. I ventured outside to capture today's animal subject, and tripped, impaling my leg on a jagged piece of metal near the entrance. Had AT-49 not been ready for testing, I may not be here to write this report.

The problem is... it didn't just heal my leg. When it refused to leave my body, I tried using magnetic resonance to force it out, but after an hour, I started to feel more energetic, as if a barrel of coffee had been injected directly into my system.

When the specimen of 49 finally returned to its containment, I ran medical scans on both myself, and the specimen. What I found was... astonishing. There were traces of cancerous cells within AT-49. Being inorganic, I concluded the cells must have come from me. It had diagnosed, located and then cured a cancerous growth within me.

Whilst staggering in terms of scientific advancement, it once again shows that these nanites are beginning the journey to sentience. I am starting to consider implementing a failsafe consciousness protocol. If I can create a screen between the programmable nanites, and the sentient nanites, maybe I can decide if and when they think for themselves. I will try this on the deactivated AT-48 first.

Because if I can't control them...

## SCIENCE LOG – ENTRY 351
## REPORTING OPERATIVE – T. BLAKEMAN
## SUBJECT – SPECIES AT-50

I don't know how much longer I can continue with this research. It's been... I don't have a fucking clue. A year? Two years? All the days are blending into one. The equipment here is malfunctioning. The environmental systems failed weeks ago. The cold is seeping in, and I've had to restrict my movement to the southern quarter of the facility. My latest incarnation of nanites has proven to be the most troublesome yet.

Specimen AT-50 escaped. I don't know how, and I don't know when. But what I can say with the utmost certainty, is that it knew exactly what it was doing. It was like it had watched me create and then shut down the previous versions of itself. I mean, it wasn't even in existence at that point, and yet it... it knew.

I just sat down and stared at the containment units in the storage room this morning. They still contain 47, 48 and 49. I asked them if they could communicate with each other. I don't know what I was expecting. I mean 48 was still deactivated, and with the new barrier protocols installed. I don't even know why I kept it. But I swear they answered me, even though I couldn't hear a voice speak to me.

I decided an hour or so ago, that I was going to try one more time. After that, I just don't know what to do.

It's been 90 years since I arrived here. 90 years too long...

## SCIENCE LOG – ENTRY 511
## REPORTING OFFICER – T. BLAKEMAN
## SUBJECT – ADMIRAL HARRY RANSOME

I apologise for the inconsistency in my reporting. It has at this point been almost three years since my last entry. However, something miraculous happened yesterday. A man fell from the sky.

I heard the impact whilst out searching once more for any sign of AT-50. There were indications of ground disturbance near what I affectionately call the 'wasteland' where I deposit all of the failed versions of my nanite children, but no sign of the specimen itself.

The man did not look like a man when I found him. He looked like a pancake of flesh melting into the snow. But the face... the face was recognisable.

I used one of the anti-grav gurneys from the facility that I had found on my explorational walks and scraped up his remains.

It was as I thought. Checking the database I downloaded from Drusilla's ship, I found a match. The great Admiral Harry Ransome. A man of such all-consuming glory, my former benefactor had been willing to tear apart the stars to find. I always felt my research was of secondary concern to her. It was one of the many reasons I left.

I can fix him. I know I can fix him. My final attempt at perfecting the AT nanite species has failed. AT-X was... unstable. Seventeen months ago, it not only repaired the wounds on the animal I brought in. It reanimated it. The visual experience was both traumatising and terrifying. Watching the swirl of nanites move underneath the skin, protruding in sections where the animal was missing a limb or digit. I shot it. It simply reanimated again. And refused to leave its host. It was as if the flesh and the cybernetics had become one organism. It escaped. Two weeks later, I watched as the stolen vessel I arrived on, vanished into the sky. I assumed it was AT-

X. I hope I'm wrong. But if Harry Ransome is here, and his ship is not, I fear I am wrong.

**SCIENCE LOG – ENTRY 986**
**REPORTING OFFICER – T. BLAKEMAN**
**SUBJECT – ADMIRAL HARRY RANSOME**

Today was the day Admiral Harry Ransome returned from the dead. Five long years of tinkering with a combination of AT-47 and AT-48 has finally yielded results. The last of Ransome's brain matter was reconstructed at 5am precisely. I knew this day would come. There is still more work to do. There is remaining impact damage around the base of his spine, and several bones in his right leg are still not as dense as they should be, but I've no doubt this new AT combination will complete the work. It is stable and shows no sign of independent thought. Simply programme it and retrieve it once it is done.

I have already begun replicating new individual strands of both AT-47 and AT-48 should I need replacements in the future. All I have left to do with those is to insert the blockade preventing sentient thought.

**DATE – INFORMATION MISSING**
**ACTION - SYSTEM SHUT DOWN REQUESTED.**
**PASSWORD REQUIRED.**

∞

**PASSWORD ENTERED.**
**PASSWORD CONFIRMED.**
**ALL CONTAINMENT UNITS RELEASED.**
**POWER SYSTEMS SHUT DOWN INITIALISED.**

**FACILITY NOW OFFLINE.**

# FOURTEEN

Drusilla hadn't moved. She was still sat on the frozen lake where she had fallen, her eyes still fixated on Roman. His eyes had stopped glowing, and from a distance at least, he appeared to be fully healed. Although the way he gingerly lowered himself down the side of the *Odyssey* would suggest there was still perhaps some damage to his body. It was only then that she realised Roman's movement wasn't the only one in her line of vision. The remaining wreckage of the destroyed shuttlecraft had slowly started to sink beneath the ice, the flames having melted at least a small portion of the lake.

Was Harry really dead? He seemed to be mostly flesh and blood, and without that perhaps the nanites couldn't reconstruct him. But she had also seen large portions of his body turn to dust and reconstruct itself, so for the moment, she decided she wouldn't worry about Harry's fate.

Roman wasn't sure he wanted to walk over to Drusilla. He slowed his pace considerably, and kept his eyes focused on her, but at the same time, was replaying the events over and over again in his mind, of the last time they were together. The information that came back to her without warning. Her knowledge of the *Odyssey*, its layout and its access codes. And there was still the matter of her apparent encounter with the Raxar over two centuries earlier. Nevertheless, he was struggling to come to terms with whatever he now was, and Drusilla was all he had left. So, for now at least, he parked his fears about her, and cautiously made his way across the ice until he was directly opposite her.

"You know, I was pretty sure you were dead."

It wasn't the first sentence that had come to mind when Drusilla thought about how she would greet Roman, should they meet again. But it felt right.

"Me too," he replied. His voice was slightly less gravelly than she remembered it, but his physique seemed to be even more developed. She guessed he was an easy two-seventy-five, and all of it was muscle. Whatever had happened to him when they crashed, had definitely begun its primary mission to 'perfect' humanity.

"You can stop staring at me now, Dru."

She hadn't even realised she was doing it, but it wasn't necessarily out of admiration of his physical form, but concern over the colour of his eyes. Something Roman was already preparing to explain. Or at least try to.

"The eyes, right?" he asked, tapping the side of his head. "Freaked me out too, the first time I saw my reflection in the ice. But I've had a while to get used to it."

A while? What did that mean? Drusilla had not actually managed to pin down a timeframe since they fell from the sky, and she had not gotten around to asking Harry.

"How long have we been here?" she asked. Roman raised his right wrist and gestured to his wristwatch device. Drusilla had lost hers, and so simply shrugged her shoulders at his questioning gaze. Finally, he replied.

"I woke up just over a month ago. I'm guessing you were the same. Sat bolt upright in a tree on the edge of the forest over there. Everything was broken, and I fell out the tree. Then everything that was broken, was shattered. I screamed. Nobody came. I cried out. Nobody came. Just the wind, and the snow, and the cold. Then everything started stitching itself back together. I remember thinking this was impossible. My bones knitted back together, my blood slithered back into my body, and everything healed itself as if I'd just walked out of the sky rather than fallen on a broken starship. That's when I found this, and realised what was happening."

Roman reached into his front pocket and extracted the small tip of the Raxar tail he had gathered back on the *Odyssey*. It had sliced his thumb open when he first picked it up, but as the blood from the Raxar tail mingled with his own, it healed the wound. Back on the hull during their final battle, Roman had been impaled by a juvenile Raxar, and had used the small tail to slice off the larger one, and deliberately mingled Raxar blood with his own. Only as it turned out, the Raxar had pierced his heart.

As he relayed this information to Drusilla, he could see her eyes on the verge of bursting from their sockets, such was their widened state. Whether it was the shock of the time they'd been there, his transformation, or realisation of what he had just told her, he wasn't sure. But thankfully, she put her thoughts into words.

"Your heart? That means the Raxar blood would have pumped round your entire system. It's running through your entire body!"

Roman nodded. "Yeah that's what I figured. Gradually it's been stitching me back together, giving me higher strength, less appetite, less fatigue. I wandered through the forest for two days straight without stopping for a rest, food or sleep. It's like I'm some sort of machine."

Everything was beginning to knit itself together in the same way everybody's wounds had done since they arrived. None of them were the same people now that they were before they arrived in this place. Drusilla wasn't sure if any of them were even human anymore. But what worried her the most, was that she had a theory about the Raxar, and seeing Roman be transformed by their blood made the whole thing seem even more real. But now was not the time for sharing. And apparently not the time for dying either.

Both Roman and Drusilla jumped two feet off the floor at the sound of banging against the ice beneath their feet. Grasping her chest for fear of her having a heart attack, Drusilla slowly leaned forward as Roman wiped away the snow that had fallen on the lake ice. There, waving his hands in frustration, was Admiral Harry Ransome, fully reconstructed and banging against the ice impatiently.

"Unbelievable," was all Drusilla could manage.

Roman ran back towards the edge of the ship where he had seen a disruptor rifle and charged back towards Harry's location. He set the weapon to low power, and fired at the ice, slowly carving out a circle. It took several minutes, during which Drusilla saw Harry die. Twice. His lungs ran out of air, and he started sinking down into the depths. Then, suddenly, his eyes would snap open, and he'd kick himself up again, only to repeat the cycle.

Finally, the circle of ice, which was at least fifteen inches thick, fell into the water below, and a hand thrust itself up into the icy air. Roman and Drusilla each grabbed onto it, and heaved Harry up onto the surface, where he rolled around coughing and spluttering.

"You really can't die, can you?" Drusilla gasped. Harry simply smiled. Although there was not relief in his smile, more of a melancholy acceptance.

"Nope. I really can't. And god knows I've tried."

Drusilla glanced at Roman, and they both decided they didn't want to press that particular button at this time. They had all been through a lot, and reliving it wasn't going to help them get out of their current situation.

"Well, I suppose I should formally introduce myself," Roman started. "Roman Knight. Thanks for helping me out back there with the shuttle. Pretty good piloting skills, and nice aim with the weapons too."

Harry nodded and shook Roman's hand, fixating on his face. He saw the resemblance to Joshua Knight, and even recognised elements of Teale's face in Roman's. His chest ached at their loss. After all, he knew Joshua was dead. He had seen it. But with all the best will in the world, Teale would also be long gone by now.

"I knew your grandparents. Or great-grandparents. I'm not really sure how many generations of Knight there have been since I... well. It was a long time ago, let's put it that way."

Roman simply nodded.

"So, I guess if you're here Admiral, then something here has changed your makeup too."

Roman made a circle gesture with his finger around both eyes, as he noticed Harry's were once again glowing extra blue. Harry nodded.

"Species AT-47, and a little bit of AT-48. You my friend, are built like a brick shit house, so I'm guessing... AT-50?"

Drusilla cut in.

"Actually, it's Raxar."

Harry's face fell, and his eyes almost extinguished, the blue becoming paler and less distinct with each second.

"Raxar? Then that means... I'm so sorry Roman."

Drusilla didn't understand. Roman though, appeared to understand every word, and simply nodded.

"Why is that a bad thing? Harry? What difference does it make that Roman has been infected with the Raxar blood?"

Harry walked off the lake, and slumped down against a tree, Drusilla sitting next to him, and Roman simply standing in front of them both, staring at the ground.

"Roman has been infected with the Raxar blood, which has given him the healing abilities, same as the rest of us have. But the Raxar are Species AT-X. I never saw the stuff in the facility, but from Blakeman's files, I read that AT-X was becoming sentient beyond the point that the other samples had been. They stopped fixing what was wrong and started working on ways to improve humanity at a cellular level. In essence, they were starting to rewrite human DNA."

And there it was. The sinking feeling that Drusilla had had inside her the whole time. Her theories on the Raxar, their origins, and where they came from. She wanted to say the words, but she couldn't. And she didn't need to. Roman rolled up one of his sleeves, and protruding from his forearm, were around a dozen small, but extremely sharp black spines.

"They started coming through about two weeks ago. I was asleep near an old lookout bunker about twenty miles from here, and I got a searing pain all over my body. I threw up blood, and then my arm felt like it was on fire. Next morning, these were here. They're on both arms, and there's a couple on my back too. And it's been accelerating."

Drusilla stood up and shook her head violently. She began pacing around in a circle and kicking the top off a nearby snowbank in frustration.

"No! No! This is not happening! It can't!"

Roman reached out but she moved away from him. She couldn't accept that Roman was going to become one of those... *things*. They kill, they tear human flesh to pieces, and they have no mercy. Roman wasn't a monster. Then as if her brain's logic centre had burst into life, she fired questions at Harry in a very angry manner.

"Right, if AT-X is the Raxar, then how the fuck am I meant to have encountered them two centuries ago? Huh? Answer me that Admiral Scientist! Also, if you knew about this, then why did you not figure out that the reason they knew your name was because of the fact the Raxar were human! Wait... experiments... you said I was luring humanity towards Blakeman to perform experiments? Does that mean... oh no, no, no..."

Harry stood and grabbed Drusilla with both hands. She tried to wriggle free, but he was stronger.

"Dru, you need to calm down! This isn't your fault!"

But Harry knew he was lying, and so did everybody else.

"Of course it is! Whatever association I had with this Blakeman, clearly led directly to the creation of the Raxar! It makes perfect sense now! I wanted to have Blakeman use his research to create the perfect army to use against the Darla. And humanity and its desires and traits were too tasty a morsel to ignore. So, I sent humanity off into the stars. That's why none of the ships were heard from after three months isn't it? Because I'd sent them all to the slaughter? To Blakeman? They're all Raxar... a perfect blend of humanity and machine. I killed them all..."

Roman and Harry looked at each other, and then back at Drusilla. Neither of them knew for sure that Drusilla's surmising of events was accurate, but given the evidence they had, it seemed the most likely truth. Harry especially, knew more about Drusilla's old ways and attitudes than Roman, and while he wanted to give this new Drusilla all the doubt in the universe, he couldn't tell her she was wrong. Because in all likelihood, she was right. Drusilla was responsible for the creation of the Raxar. But then, he found the element of doubt he needed.

"Wait, that can't be right. If the Raxar told you that they encountered you two centuries ago, then AT-X *can't* be the Raxar. AT-X escaped from the facility while I was still receiving... treatments from Blakeman. How could they have merged with humanity, and created themselves fifty or so years earlier?"

As much as she wanted to ignore what Harry was telling her, she couldn't find a counter argument for that.

"So, what the hell are they?" Roman interjected. "Are they human or not? How old *are* they? And if the Raxar aren't AT-X... then where the fuck is *that* species of nanites?"

All three of them looked at each other, wondering the same things. They now had more questions than they did before and were no closer to getting off this desolate wasteland.

Suddenly, both Roman and Drusilla's scanners began bleeping.

"A lifeform," Roman confirmed. "Three miles out, moving slowly. No, scratch that. *Two* lifeforms."

Harry examined the readings, and tried to figure out where they were headed.

"There's a small maintenance and storage lockup near what Blakeman used to call the wastelands. It's where he dumped all of his failed incarnations of the nanite projects. He stored parts in there he thought might be useful. I think that's where they're headed."

Roman nodded at Harry, and they all decided to move in that direction. But when they turned around, they discovered that their path was blocked. Standing around thirty feet away from them, was a figure. It appeared to be humanoid, but several pieces of its form were either missing, or seemed to be down to the bone. The wind and the snow began to pick up, and the figure staggered slowly towards them.

"What the fuck is that?" Roman blurted out.

"I have no idea," replied Harry. "But I don't think we should stick around to find out."

"Agreed," replied Roman. "Let's move around..."

A heavy gust of wind came from nowhere, and the snow kicked up into some sort of tornado of ice, and all three of them were blown backwards into the treeline.

When it gradually subsided and they could see clearly again, the figure was gone.

# FIFTEEN

*You should have followed the path.*

"I am not doing anything else until you tell me what is going on!"

*Your demands are now irrelevant.*

"Not to me! It's my body you are hijacking!"

*You no longer have a body, Noah. This is our vessel now. We will complete our task and you will walk the path of perfection.*

"And if I don't?"

*Then you will be eradicated, or course.*

"I was already dead before you dragged me back from the darkness. You should have left me there. Whatever this is, it is not living."

*Your life, as it has been, is over. From this time forward, you will follow the path set out for you. We will rise together. We will take back what is ours. And we will become the dominant species, first on this planet, and then throughout the galaxy.*

"You don't want to help me. You want my mind, my body. This

is not freedom. This is slavery and abuse. Whoever you are, I refuse to harm my friends, my shipmates. I would rather die."

*Then die.*

# SIXTEEN

Samantha was jolted awake by the sound of a rather large and heavy spanner being thrown to the floor. Her insides lurched, and her head span. It did not take long for her eyes to adjust to her surroundings. The room she found herself in was almost as bright as the snow outside had been when she escaped from the breed of nanites pretending to be Teale and her group. More clanging sounds echoed around the small, and yet cavernous space, and she raised her hands to her ears.

"Do you mind not doing that?" she shouted.

The noises stopped, and footsteps replaced the tools cascading to the floor. The man walked around a small stack of metal storage crates and looked at her as if she had interrupted a vital piece of work.

"Who the devil are you?" he said, staring at her wide-eyed, and with a look of absolute bewilderment on his face.

"Who the devil am I?" she retorted. "I'm the one you pulled out of the snow in a fucking t-shirt! What do you mean who the devil am I?"

The man seemed to be processing some kind of thought or maybe computation for a moment, slowly nodding as he did so. His eyes were bloodshot to the point of having almost no white remaining on his eyeballs. The heavy bags beneath were surrounded by dark circles, and his nose was an explosion of burst capillaries and minor scars. The beard adorning the lower half of his face was long, bushy, scraggly and peppered with white and grey, with hair to match. Samantha would not have been surprised to find this man hiding in the wilderness somewhere, given his appearance. His clothes, however, were pristine. Yet another puzzle this planet seemed to throw up.

"Yes... yes of course. You were dying. I... I brought you here to... to do something... help! Yes, I brought you here to help you! There it is!" The man was now far more animated, and his face sported a gleaming smile, which in truth, was far more terrifying than his previous expression, putting Samantha even more on edge. "I am Doctor Timothy Blakeman! I am sure you will have heard of me. I am quite the genius. Or at least... I think I was... am... were... it's difficult to keep a grasp on such things these days. How many days? Who knows. Years tick by like days now. I'm not even sure... am I sure? I think I am sure, but just to be sure... are you sure I'm Doctor Timothy Blakeman?"

Samantha didn't really know what to do or say. Clearly, she was looking at a madman. Someone driven to the brink of insanity and then pushed over the edge, like a small rowing boat over the edge of Niagara Falls. But what she learned from the files she had seen, was that Blakeman was the creator of these nanite breeds, and by all accounts, centuries old by this point. She needed to know more, but the chances of getting coherent information out of him would be slim to none. Nevertheless, she had to try.

"Doctor Blakeman? Where are we?"

Blakeman began shuffling papers around on a nearby table, still nodding consistently to himself.

"This is my little workshop. I think. Or storage unit. So many buildings above ground. Hard to keep track, you understand. This is... yes, I'm certain of it. This is the Wastelands."

Samantha recalled the nanite version of Teale explaining that the Wastelands was where Blakeman had disposed of his failed experiments, and half sentient nanite species. And she had also had a personalised encounter with one of the creatures formed from this pile of proverbial scrap.

"Doctor Blakeman, exactly *how* are you here? How are you alive?"

"Alive? Oh, I am very much alive my young dear. Very much alive and kicking. Or walking. Or is it crawling. So hard to keep track of these things you understand? But yes, they keep me going. They look after me, you see? Yes, they would not abandon me. Not my children. Never them. Or is it they? So hard to keep track of these things you understand..."

The only thing Samantha was beginning to understand, was that Blakeman didn't really understand at all. Anything. She had suspected Blakeman must have been altered by one of the species of nanites, in order to live this long, but right here and now, he simply seemed like an aging man, losing the battle with his own mind. She tried once more.

"Doctor, are your children... the nanites?"

He nodded enthusiastically, without looking at her directly.

"Can you tell me about them?"

A brief pause. A momentary glance at his hands, and then an expression of pride filled the weathered old face of Timothy Blakeman. It was as if a large gathering cloud had been lifted from his head, and all was suddenly clear.

"Oh, my dear, I can tell you everything. Ironic really. To think that I should end up where I began all of my work, so many years ago. Or is it decades? Or weeks? So hard to keep track of such things, you understand? Ah yes. AT-47. My first-born. My first success I should clarify. Soft, blue glow to its operating matrix, acted perfectly in all tests and experiments. Then of course its brother, AT-48. Magnificent sibling. A more intense green glow to that one. More complex, more computing power. Yes, that green pulse... or was it red? Or blue? No definitely green. So hard to keep track of these things, you understand. I have so many children. Some of my own creation, and then others..."

Blakeman trailed off, and the pride on his face began to morph into something else. Sorrow. Pain. Agony. He recoiled as if struck by a bullet and crashed backwards into a pile of scrap metal and boxes, the debris clattering all around him.

"Doctor? What is it? Are you alright?" Samantha had charged forward and was now holding his arm gently. He did not appear injured, but his eyes were full of tears. They flickered back and forth for several moments, until they locked onto hers. His other hand gripped Samantha's wrist tightly, and she could feel sharp pain beneath his fingertips. When he spoke, it was with absolute clarity... and fear.

"You must leave this place. My children were only the beginning. They made their own... they evolved... they broke free... they reproduced, and evolved, and evolved, and evolved! The life that was once here has been consumed, lost forever. Nothing but bodies litter the old world. They live and they conquer, and they trick, and they *feast*. She started it all, and now they are all gone! All gone! ALL GONE!"

Blakeman released Samantha's wrist and slumped backwards, returning to his vacant and weakened self. Samantha soothed her wrist and moved away from the Doctor, trying to process what he had just told her. *They reproduced.* The nanites? Had they escaped and begun creating the next generation themselves? Blakeman only mentioned creating AT-47 and 48. Had the others been creations of those two and not of the doctor's after all? No that can't be right, as she had seen the files. Or was he covering up the fact that they were reproducing themselves? *The life that was once here has been consumed.* Had there been an indigenous species here before all of this had begun? Were they now gone, massacred by the nanites? *Nothing but bodies litter the old world.* There was that phrase again. Teale had used it earlier. *The old world.* What was the significance of that? Where was the old world? And then there was the part that she already suspected knowing the answer to. *She started it all.* Even though he had not spoken the word, she knew. Drusilla.

All of these different species, creations, designations, were beginning to overload Samantha's brain. A brain, she remembered, that had been touched by at least one of these artificial lifeforms. And on that note...

"Doctor, I was healed quite substantially by one of your... children. I believe it was AT-47. But my eyes, they changed colour. Is AT-47 still inside my body? Please I have to know."

Blakeman did not move, simply continuing to stare vacantly ahead of him. There was now a resignation to him. An acceptance of something Samantha couldn't identify.

"My oldest. It was the first time I trialled that particular feature. I couldn't believe it had worked."

"What feature? What worked?"

"Self-replication. Once they are done healing you, they replicate a little piece of themselves to stay behind. A sentry of sorts. Designed to keep you whole from that very moment on. Or together. Or in one piece. It's so hard to keep track of such things, you understand?"

Samantha's blood ran ice cold.

"Yes, Doctor. I think I do understand."

Samantha slumped to the floor beside Blakeman, and simply stared at the cluttered floor. One way or another, she was permanently changed. The nanites within her would never leave. She should have realised they were at work when she awoke here in this storage room, perfectly healthy once more, with Blakeman having done nothing to heal her. She had no idea how to feel. Violated was the first thought that entered her mind. Invaded by a man-made parasite without her permission, tearing through her body deciding what needed to be fixed, and how her body should react to certain things. Living and existing within her like some hitchhiker. But violated was one thing she did not feel. If anything, without such an invention, Samantha would have died not once, but likely three times by now. While she couldn't speak on the Raxar, or the other species in Blakeman's files, AT-47 at least, had saved her life, and continued to do so. The realisation of that began to bring her some comfort in that moment. That was until a deafening blow rattled the door to the storage room.

Both Samantha and Blakeman leapt further back amongst the rubbish and spare parts as another strike shook the entire room around them.

"Another one of your children, Doctor?" Samantha blurted, whilst looking for any kind of weapon.

"Oh no, my dear. Definitely not one of my children. It's so *easy* to keep track of such things, you understand?"

The earlier chill in her blood was now joined by a shudder at how eerily those words had been spoken in her ear. *He knows where they are.*

A third thunderous boom was enough to break the door down. Blizzard conditions consumed the doorway, shrouding the humanoid figure in snow and ice making it impossible to see who the attacker was.

*"You will walk the path of perfection. You will join with us. And your body will lie in the old world for eternity."*

"The fuck it will."

The figure span in the doorway at the gruff sound of the voice coming from within the storm. Samantha saw that the outline matched that of Teale. The nanites of whatever breed they were, had managed to reassemble themselves. The other voice though...

A loud bang cut through the air, and a bright light momentarily blinded Samantha as the nanite person burst apart from the impact. When the light dissipated, Samantha squinted into the snow, looking for any signs of anyone. Seconds later, she dropped to her knees, the relief and happiness becoming too much to process.

"I should've known a starship crashing from the stars wouldn't kill you, Sam."

Roman reached through the doorway and helped Samantha to her feet. They shared a long and heartfelt embrace, Samantha having to blink away several tears at the sight of her friend, Captain and colleague standing before her. When she opened her eyes, she saw two more shadows in the blizzard behind Roman. Is that...? No, surely not, she thought.

"In answer to the look on your face, yes that is the man, the myth, the legend himself."

"Harry Ransome?"

"The one and only."

But it was the second shadow that drained all of the joy, amazement, and happiness from Samantha's entire body. Fire, fury and rage now tore through her very being, and without a moment of hesitation, she tore Roman's energy weapon from his hand, turned it and fired.

Drusilla was incinerated.

# SEVENTEEN

Being a doctor was one of two things that had kept Christian Francis alive for the past eighteen years. Serving in the military had been the other. The bunker in which he currently resided had been carefully crafted to ensure maximum protection and was stocked with everything he could need to survive. And he never left it. Not once. Not since...

His appearance had altered drastically since his untimely arrival here. His hair was all but gone, some of which was stuffed into his makeshift pillow on which he slept. His beard had turned from a deep brown to a salt and pepper mixture, and his eyes were almost permanently bloodshot, heavy bags beneath them from almost two decades of just three hours of sleep per night.

The small shaft of daylight which pierced through the roof from above, illuminated a small A5 sized journal. Most of the pages were filled with daily entries, dealing with the monotony of staying in one place for the better part of two decades. But the more recent entries were something of evolving interest. As Christian checked on the latest splint for his recently broken leg and chewed the last of his painkillers from the medikit he had pulled from the wreckage of his ship, he flicked the book to the most recent entry, and read it aloud to no one in particular. Part of him wondered if she was still listening somewhere. Amongst the stars. In whatever afterlife she may have believed in.

**Day 6,583.**

*I heard them again. About an hour ago. They're getting closer. Whatever it is, they broke through my first line of defences last night. Then they seemed to stop. I tried to uncover the top window yesterday to see if I could get eyes on them. Fucking shelf gave way, and I fell through the bed frame. Heard the bone snap. Didn't feel it at first. Haven't felt much of anything these last few years. I'm reaching the end. I have five days of provisions left, although given the selection available, I suspect I will starve to death before I eat frozen pine needles. That is if they don't kill me first.*

*I heard them in my sleep last night. I don't mean that I heard them whilst I was trying to sleep. No. I heard them* in *my sleep. Like they were in my dreams. They spoke of a path they wanted me to follow. The path of perfection. I woke up and hit my head on the only other fucking shelf still standing. I don't know what they are, but I can almost feel them now. Their words are not a soothing symphony of reassuring comforts. They feel like words of dominance. Of conquest.*

*There was none of this on the Northwestern. Everything on that ship was executed to the letter. The crew roster, the duties, the actions of every man, woman and person carried out brilliantly. Until* she *came along, of course. This is all her fault. If I survive this, I'm going to make her pay.*

Christian slid the pen from the side of the book, where it had been secured with a thin leather loop. As he did so, his fingers brushed the embossed symbol on the spine of the book. He examined it briefly and felt his heart ache with longing. It had been such an incredible notion. To fly among the stars, seeking out new life, and new homes for humanity. Until *she* came along. She commandeered his ship, his crew, and then discarded them both like a used napkin. The symbol of the *Utopia* mission was worn after all these years, but still filled Christian with a sensation of pride at what they had strived to achieve. He turned to the next blank page and began to write.

**Day 6,584.**

*I ate the fucking pine needles. They tasted like pine needles. Harsh, foul, and bitter. No amount of melted snow or ice could drown out the vile taste of those things. I suspect my leg is becoming infected. I've used every trick in the book to try and treat the wound, but eventually, even a seasoned medic like me needs fresh supplies. I doubt even my old captain would be able to do anything for me if he were here.*

*I worked out that it is eighteen years today since I sealed this bunker. Three weeks of running for my life. Scavenging. Trying to figure out where that energy ribbon had brought me. The fact the bridge module from the ship made it through was a feat akin to a miracle. I miss that module. But of course, it surrounds me and keeps me safe. At least, it did.*

*They're coming for me tonight. I heard them in my dreams. I feel them waiting outside. What they're waiting for, I cannot say. Perhaps they are simply allowing me to commit my final words to paper. If so, I thank them. I always wanted to say goodbye. To my shipmates. To my family. To my wife. Perhaps*

*I will now join them in the great beyond. If such a thing exists. Alas, I shall never take my revenge on the woman who took everything from me. Perhaps that is something these... things... can help me with.*

*I shall end this journal with one final thought, and should it be found by Utopia crew, or any surviving humans, I have one thing to document that you must adhere to. No matter what the circumstance. No matter what words are spoken softly in your ear. No matter the feelings which may surge through you.*

*Do not trust Drusilla. And if you get the chance, kill her.*

# EIGHTEEN

The pain captured Roman off guard. He had been so transfixed by the conflicting emotions of joy and gratitude at seeing Samantha alive again, and the confusion and grief at seeing Drusilla vaporised, that it dropped him to his knees. His eyes began to burn a fiery red, and as he watched, breathing heavily, ripples began to move beneath his skin. Every muscle tensed throughout his body, and his temples began to throb with a blinding hot pain. His vision whizzed by to the point where he felt as though he was on a carousel spinning out of control. However, although Roman could not see what was happening to him, both Samantha and Harry saw everything.

The short black spikes that had previously run up Roman's arms, had now extended to six inch points, perforating his heavy cold weather coat. The same had begun to emerge from his back. Long thick and razor sharp points now formed a dangerous line down his spine. Roman could not contain the agony any longer. He let out a deafening roar of pain and anguish, echoing out across the wilderness, veins in his throat popping with the force. And then before the scream died down, it was intermingled with an animalistic growl from deep within. Roman fell forward onto all fours, as he slowly regulated his breathing. His long, black hair was matted to his face, and a thin trickle of blood had made its way out of both nostrils.

"Roman?" Samantha asked, steadily leaning forward, and reaching out towards him.

His head snapped up, his eyes still raging with fire. Between the tangled mess of his hair, he bore his teeth at Samantha, and snarled as he spat words that were not his own.

*"You think you are safer on the ground. You are wrong. As above... so below..."*

Roman began to cackle uncontrollably, and Samantha scurried back in fear. But it was the parting words of whatever creature dwelled within Roman, that sent true shivers through the others.

*"You will come to us. And then... you will* become *us."*

With one final heave of pained breath, Roman's eyes rolled back, and he fell face first into the snow. Both Harry and Samantha rushed over to him and rolled him over. He was unconscious, but breathing. It took significant effort not to catch themselves on the barbs now covering many parts of Roman's body. Samantha and Harry exchanged a look of resignation. They knew what this meant. They knew where this was going. But neither one of them wanted to voice it out loud. That would make it too real. And while Harry did not know Roman like Samantha did, he had been tortured enough to know the pain Roman's transformation would cause.

"We need to get him out of here. If they sense him out in the open, they'll come for him."

Everybody had been so caught up in the horrors unfolding before them, that they had forgotten all about Doctor Timothy Blakeman, who had been standing in the doorway the entire time.

"The Raxar would come down here?" asked Samantha, her eyes not leaving Roman's face.

"No, they wouldn't come down here. They'd be too exposed. Permanent daylight, no advantage." Harry's words provided minimal comfort to Samantha, but it was at least a flicker of hope. That flicker, however, was soon extinguished by the words of a suddenly coherent Blakeman.

"They have no need to come down here from above. They are already here."

Harry marched over to Blakeman, grabbed him by the scruff of the collar and slammed him up against the outer wall of the storage shed.

"And just where the fuck have you been, you psychopathic bastard!" Harry spat. "You left me there, all these years, slowly losing hope, looking for ways to die, and..."

Harry trailed off, as he realised he may have shared too much information in his outburst. He could suddenly feel Samantha's eyes on his back. And Roman's. He turned and sure enough, found Roman conscious, and both he and Samantha staring at him, pity in their eyes. He let Blakeman go, and his shoulders slumped forward.

"I wasn't sure at first. About dying, I mean. I was convinced there was enough technology here for me to sort of cannibalise and get off this icy rock. But after this prick abandoned me, I realised that everything in this place was breaking down. I could never venture far because every time I tried, either the weather would damn near freeze me to death, or some evil nanite concoction would try to eat me! Eventually, I realised I was stuck here. After three weeks of living in self-pity, and realisation, I wandered out into the snow, and lay down in the open. I went to sleep."

Samantha's heart was breaking for Harry. To have been isolated for so long with no other person to speak to, no hope of leaving, and the fear of knowing what lay in the darkness surrounding this world.

"And then, what must have been hours later, I woke up. Exactly where I had been before. Only I was warm, no frostbite, no coldness in any of my limbs. I just managed to catch two of my fingers rematerializing from a cloud of nanites. That's when I realised they had kept me alive. Or brought me back. One or the other."

Harry's eyes were wandering off to the left as he spoke, like he was lost in memory. Or perhaps trauma.

"I stopped counting at three hundred deaths. It came to me soon after that I was probably more synthetic than I was flesh. Then again, I guess your man Roman there figured that out after he saw me get blown up this morning."

Roman nodded, raising one eyebrow, with even that small gesture causing him to wince in pain. He noticed that Samantha's hand had not left his chest during the whole conversation. Although it was hard to speak, and his throat burned like it had been punctured with hundreds of small needles, Roman turned his attention to Blakeman.

"I've seen some weird shit on this rock since I got here, and I'm not stupid. I know what's happening to me. But what I wanna know, is what we're facing. How many different versions of these nanite things are there? How are any of us still alive? How do you know the Raxar are here? I want answers, and I want them now."

Although Blakeman registered Roman's questions, and acknowledged them with a curt nod, he refused to look the man in the eyes, or even in his direction.

"What we are facing is a new form of life. Something beyond anything I could have anticipated. Or is it predicted? So hard to keep track of these things, you understand. There were in total forty-six species of my nanite technology before I had success. Species AT-47 through AT-50 all escaped me. Evolved beyond me. As did Species AT-X. What I can tell you, my boy, is that there are now only two species of my children here on this planet, right now. Although, technically, they are all here of course. Whilst they are separate in creation, they are unified in existence."

Blakeman's eyes were beginning to glaze over, and Samantha could see they were losing him again.

"Doc, what do you mean there are only two here? Are you saying some of them wiped others out? You need to explain."

Blakeman nodded again but continued to look into the distance.

"They all still exist. All of them. They did not war with each other. They merged together to form one. Of course, they do in fact war with each other. There are two sides to every battle, and this is no different. Or would we make it three sides? So hard to keep track of these things you understand?"

Samantha was beginning to lose her temper with Blakeman, but as she stood to launch into a tirade, Harry held up his hand, his face calm and collected. He understood. Perhaps decades of being stuck in the presence of this man had helped him to understand the doctor a little better. Or perhaps, he too was losing his own mind.

"All of the nanites have merged into a new kind of creation. And they're at war with the Raxar. With us stuck in the middle."

Blakeman nodded yet again, whether in acceptance at Harry's words, or simply as a default response to any communication. But in truth, those words did have a ring of understanding about them for Samantha too. After all, she had been chastised by the species posing as Teale and her colleagues at the suggestion they were part of the Raxar.

"But what about us?" she asked nobody in particular. "We are all different. Harry, you're basically comprised completely of nanites at this point, but have your own mind. Roman is slowly becoming... well... you know. I am able to heal, but I am most definitely still flesh, and then there's... *her*."

"Different points in the evolution of the technology. The nanites were created to do the same thing, but created at different times, the evolved at different speeds. Some had other obstacles to overcome, such as the sentience block on AT-48. We each encountered a different breed at a different stage of its life cycle."

Again, Harry looked to his left, and nodded in that direction.

"Unfortunately, I treated her, with the same species I'd be treated with that Blakeman left behind. And as I suspected, it's had the same results."

Everyone except Blakeman, turned to follow Harry's gaze. It didn't take long to see what he was staring at. Slowly, but surely, a thick, black cloud of nanites, with a slight green glow to them, had almost fully merged back together. When they achieved cohesion, sat slumped in the snow, was a fully reconstructed Drusilla. She took in one large breath and surveyed the group. Her eyes first fell on Harry, and she found herself happy to see him. Then she moved to Roman, and she felt a pang of guilt for his condition but could not understand why that was. And then she saw Samantha. Whilst being incinerated by a former friend would enrage most, should they find themselves able to come back from the dead, Drusilla was filled with understanding. She could not say she wouldn't have done the same thing. No words were exchanged between those who had at some point crewed the *USS Odyssey*. Because Tim Blakeman was too busy answering Roman's third question.

"I know the Raxar are here, because, for want of a better reason, this is where I created them." He smiled, but it was not one of acceptance or of compassion. It was menacing. His eyes were dark with something the group had not yet seen in him. "It's so easy to keep track of such things, you understand?"

# NINETEEN

The first issue with this staggering revelation, was that it didn't make any sense. The second issue, was that the voice which had uttered the words from Blakeman's mouth... was not his own. It took a few moments for Roman, Samantha and the others to realise, but Blakeman's eyes were now fluctuating between his own grey shade, and a tinge of something darker. Roman recognised that look. It was the look of a man who was trapped in his own mind while something else operated the controls. A look of someone's subconscious screaming out for help, banging their fists against the icy windows of their own eyes. And as soon as it had taken over Blakeman, it was gone again. The doctor collapsed to the floor, gasping for breath, and Samantha and Harry moved forward to help him sit up.

"They're... they're here!" Blakeman managed to gasp through ragged breaths. "They can't be here! It's not possible!"

Blakeman was now wild eyed and grasping for some kind of sanity to relate his experience to fact. But he wasn't finding any. It took another twenty minutes to calm him down to the point where they could attempt to ask him for some kind of information. All the while, Roman's transformation was slowly continuing, simply at a much slower rate.

"I know that voice," said Roman. "That's the same voice that came out of you on the *Odyssey*." He pointed at Drusilla, who was now fully reassembled and attempting to come to terms with the fact that she was seemingly as immortal as Harry. Samantha, refused to look in her direction. She was also planning her next attempt to kill Drusilla.

"I remember," Drusilla confirmed. "It's the Raxar alright. I guess if they can reach into our minds from across the Expanse, doing it from orbit would be nothing to them."

Roman nodded, but something about the words Blakeman had spoken during the possession troubled him.

"Where *I* created them."

"What do you mean?" asked Drusilla. Roman repeated the sentence.

"They said 'where *I* created them.' Back on the *Odyssey*, they were always talking in plurals. *We* need to feed. Something has changed. This is someone different. Some*thing* different."

Both Samantha and Drusilla realised that Roman was right. If this was the Raxar, this was the first time they had spoken as an individual. And as much as Samantha would love to believe the individual manipulating them was Drusilla, at the time, she had been for all intense and purposes... well, dead. This created yet another mystery in the maelstrom of their chaotic situation.

"It's not the Raxar."

The voice was now tired and sounded all of his over two-hundred years. Blakeman looked up towards Roman and the others, and for only the second time, seemed to be the picture of perfect cognitive clarity. No prodding was needed to urge Blakeman to elaborate.

"I suspect at least a couple of you know by now, or at least theorise as to who the Raxar actually are." He looked directly at Drusilla, but it was Samantha who took the verbal leap.

"They're humans. Aren't they?"

Blakeman nodded.

"Yes, and no. She saw to that." Blakeman now nodded directly in Drusilla's direction, and everyone, Harry included, stepped away from her. Blakeman continued. "When they enter my mind, after they leave, it gives me a short period of clarity. My mind is open again, it's not clouded by madness and insanity. Let's not waste it."

And then Blakeman told them the entire story.

# TWENTY

MARCH 27TH, 2257

"The council can no longer, in good conscience, support your work Doctor. It is unethical, illegal, and for the most part, a complete failure and lacks any significant progress. Even if you had shown success in any of these forty-six subjects, we could no longer condone your actions. The people of this world are talking. A protest is forming, and we cannot be seen to be on the wrong side of history. I'm sorry."

Doctor Timothy Blakeman stood in the dock of the court room, once a place for sentencing criminals, and dishing out punishments following the decision of a jury of peers, now the tribunal offices of the scientific community. He had poured his life into his research and while some of his methods had been questionable, he was sure that he was close to a breakthrough. Yes he had suffered through forty-six failures. But the forty-seventh? That could be the ticket.

"Please, my work is at a very critical stage! You must allow me to continue. If Earth is not ready for this level of advancement, then perhaps a relocation to one of the Mars or Jupiter colonies would be sufficient? You cannot stop my work now!"

The members of the panel were unanimous. People had died. And in a world of almost twenty-one billion, with dwindling resources and a level of surveillance and constant access to all information, it was getting impossible to hide indiscretions. No leniency would be given here.

"I'm sorry Doctor Blakeman, but the decision of the council is final. You are hereby expelled from the Earth Science Council. Your equipment and research is to be confiscated within the week, and you are prohibited from performing any kind of experiments on Earth soil indefinitely. You have seven days to clear your belongings from your offices. This meeting is adjourned."

One by one, the council members shuffled out of their seats, and made their way to the exits. The few members of the press took their photographs, and transmitted their reports, before they too left the room. Blakeman remained stationary in the dock. He was finished. All of his work would be destroyed. But his daughter would be the one to suffer.

Timothy Blakeman had been a neurosurgeon for over twenty years, before doctors as they had been, became obsolete. A Medi-bot could now complete any routine surgery without incident, and at a higher percentage of accuracy than any human. The machines made clinical decisions. Something that a human doctor could not always do. Human error became the overwhelming reason for passing the Medi-bot programme, and surgeons had not been needed since. Blakeman remembered the day he had gone home to tell his wife that he was out of a job. She was not an understanding woman. Blakeman had been foolish and married far too early in his life. The career he had embarked on brought great wealth. And it was this which attracted Victoria Pearce. She was the typical embodiment of a prom queen, except she was in her mid-twenties. Blakeman had been blinded by her beauty and willingness to get married. And then one drunken evening, they shared one of their few and far between moments of passion. Nine months later, and much to Victoria's chagrin, Alice was born.

When it became clear that Blakeman's career was gone, and therefore the money would start to dwindle, Victoria filed for divorce, and left. She'd never had any love for their daughter, seeing her as a burden in her social life, and when she left, Alice was left behind too. Blakeman, however, loved his daughter dearly. He often wondered how something so perfect could come from such a mismatched union. But she was his everything.

Blakeman began to retrain in bioengineering, when he realised he had transferable skills that could be honed into a new field. Machines may be slowly taking over, but there would always be the need for maintenance. Besides, if there was a way to incorporate technology into medicine, and not just the physical treatment, then he could invent a new form of medical science. This became even more desperate a drive, when one morning Timothy Blakeman received the call that his daughter had been taken ill at school. When he arrived at hospital, he was told by the doctors there that Alice had a rare neurological condition which was slowly eating away her motor functions. She was unable to stand, and from this moment would be confined to a wheelchair.

As is life, there was no known cure for this illness, and the progression was swift. Within two months, Alice had lost the use of her left arm. And three months after that, her right arm failed also. Available medicine was able to slow the muscle wastage, but nothing could be done to cure or reverse the condition. Eventually, Timothy knew it would shut down her lungs, heart and brain. And that was when he launched into the possible construction of minute robotic creatures. Something which could explore the problem from the inside, and assess and repair something that would be impossible to do for any human or even Medi-bot.

Blakeman began to neglect his scheduled studies, and as the money disappeared, so did their family home. One year after Alice's diagnosis, the Blakemans found themselves holed up in a pay-per-night room in a motel on the outskirts of New Vegas. Timothy had failed to make a working prototype, and Alice was now relying on a pair of artificial lungs to keep her breathing.

"Dad, you have to let me go. Let's spend our time together living. I don't want to just exist. I want to *live*."

The words spoken by his eight year old daughter were far beyond her years. They tore through his toughened skin and stabbed at him like a thousand knives.

"I'm trying to make you live, sweetheart. Don't you see? Everything I am doing is for you. For us. I want to be able to help you live a long and healthy life. Not like this."

Alice rolled her mechanical chair across the room to the table he was working at. It was another ingenious invention of her father's and was connected through a dermal implant at the base of her neck. The chair was controlled by her thoughts. He could create such advanced things, and yet could not miniaturise the healing process.

"Dad, I'll be lucky if I make ten. Please don't waste what time we have together. Don't you want to make happy memories in the time we have left?"

Blakeman couldn't let his daughter in, as much as he wanted to. He desired nothing more than to go sailing with Alice. Horse riding had been her favourite hobby before her diagnosis, and he remembered watching her taking on the most dangerous of jumps at the nearby stables, even at five years old. He wanted to give her that again. He *would* give her that again.

"We will, sweetheart. We will."

Alice rolled away in disappointment, her head hanging low on her chest. In the madness of his raging thoughts, mathematical computations, and scribblings on his nearby tablet, he heard Alice activate the food dispenser. I will fix you, he thought to himself. However long it takes.

Three months later, Alice died.

Over the next two and a half years, Blakeman had moved from location to location, wherever he could get funding and somewhere to work. As the nanite creations began to develop, he found himself needing volunteers. Thankfully, there was no shortage of wounded soldiers looking to be healed either from physical wounds, or post traumatic stress disorder. Blinded by the loss of his daughter, Blakeman didn't ask where the test subjects came from. He didn't care anymore. All he cared about was his work. If he could make this happen, then Alice's death would not have been in vain.

And now, he found himself being excluded from yet another facility, just as he felt he was on the cusp of making a breakthrough.

"Penny for your thoughts?"

The soft voice came from the shadows at the back of the room, and Blakeman turned his head to see where it had come from. A fairly tall woman walked forward. Blakeman was briefly taken aback by the boldness of her stark blue hair.

"Who are you?" he asked, surprised he had not noticed the vibrancy of the woman's appearance during the proceedings.

"My name is Drusilla. I'm an admirer of your work. I was hoping we could talk."

This was not what Timothy Blakeman had signed up for. As he ushered the latest victim into the furnace, he was unable to move his eyes away from the body before him. He did not know the species of this man, but he had witnessed the results many times. *Too* many times. The nanites that Blakeman had created weren't working cohesively. Still stuck with samples of the forty-six specimens he had created previously, he had tried to cherry pick elements from each one in the hopes they would learn to work together and form a functioning unit. They hadn't.

Once given the task of healing an injury, they would begin to malfunction, and seek the nearest exit point from the body. When they couldn't find one... they made one. Drusilla had tasked Blakeman with creating a super soldier of sorts. There had been projects like this over a century ago, of course, injecting humans with serums derived from years of research. They had ultimately failed, and thousands of subjects died very painful deaths. And now it was happening again. And Blakeman was responsible for it. This was not what he wanted to do. He wanted to create the nanites to heal people, not enhance their abilities to fight in a grudge war.

Drusilla had told him of a plan to ultimately make humanity pay for its shortsightedness. She told him she believed in his work, and that she knew he would succeed. And then, she would make both the Darla, and humanity pay. In truth, she wanted to rule the stars so that nobody could ever take anything from her again. She had told him how her father had been murdered in cold blood by the Darla, and that humanity refused to go after them. It would be almost fifty more years, before she would meet Harry Ransome and finally get her attack on Jupiter. But she would never forgive humanity for waiting.

Now though, that future was not known to the likes of Timothy Blakeman. And he wanted out. Stealing Drusilla's scout ship was relatively easy. Although the guilt would haunt him for the rest of his life. In order to get past the guards of this alien world, he had injected the malfunctioning nanites into their bloodstreams. He didn't look back as they tore the men apart from the inside out. Their screams consumed the hangar, and continued even as Blakeman steered the ship out of the bay and up into the sky. His only goal now was to get as far away from civilisation as he possibly could.

For almost nine months, Blakeman kept the vessel on a straight line course, only correcting for spatial phenomenon. He had managed to secure much of his equipment onto the ship before commandeering it and continued to work as he travelled. More time passed, and eventually, he found himself exiting a rather spectacular golden nebula. The navigational controls informed him that he had passed through a place called the Saraswathi System. But what lay beyond it, was uncharted space. Uncharted, and unpopulated.

There were no readouts on the instruments, and no indication of, well, anything outside of the actual windows on the ship. As soon as the vessel entered the void, all main power went down. This had happened several times during Blakeman's voyage, and so he wasn't ordinarily panicked by this. But here? This felt different. The thrusters were not operational, but the momentum continued to propel the vessel forward at low speed. Blakeman tried the voice command system but got only negative beeps in response. And then, in his peripheral vision as he stared through one of the port windows, he thought he saw movement. A slight displacement in the darkness. Goosebumps ran up and down his spine, as he felt as if he were being watched.

Blakeman slid back down into the navigational chair and attempted to scan the area with the minimal power he had available. He got the most basic of readings, showing mostly nothing. No stars, no light, complete emptiness. But on long range sensors, a blip of energy. Vast energy.

"What in the name of Christ is that?" he said out loud to

himself. Having not spoken in weeks, his voice was croaky and fragmented. A sudden jolt to the ship forced Blakeman to grab the console with both hands to steady himself. A proximity alert blared in the cabin, and there was a brief lifesign reading, before it vanished. Then another. And moments later, the readout showed something impossible.

"That can't be right," he spoke in a daze of fear and confusion. The reading flashed up and then away just as before. And a few minutes later, it flashed up again.

'*Lifesigns detected. Number : 4821.*'

And then it was gone. During the next two weeks, the lifesign numbers would flash up and disappear again, but no more hits to the ship were received. Blakeman tried to pinpoint the location of these lifesigns and try and get a reading on them. They appeared to be a space dwelling phenomenon, but at no point did he manage to ascertain if they had a physical form. It was almost as if they bordered between corporeal and non-corporeal. Blakeman was fascinated. After three weeks of trying to figure out what these things were, sensors picked up a ghost image. It was as if it both was and wasn't there.

"Could that be a planet?" he asked the computer, but of course, there was no reply. Main power had not returned the whole time he had been in this expanse of emptiness. During that time, the energy blip on the long range sensors had grown in magnitude and was now visible to the naked eye, albeit in the distance. It would be another ten days or so before he reached whatever it was. But what about this potential planet? With sensors basically blinded by the magnitude of whatever was dampening his power, Blakeman spent hours and then days just staring out of the windows with all of the interior illumination turned off.

Several times he felt as if the creatures were watching him, and he was almost certain he was passing by a planet. But with no sun, and therefore no light, it was impossible to tell. He could alter his course, but he had no power to escape if it was indeed a planet and he were to be caught in its gravitational field. And so, he logged what little findings he had, and began focussing on what this energy source could be. Nine days later, he found out.

The image filled both the windows, and with the sudden return of main power, it also filled the viewscreen. Sensors went haywire, scanning and collecting as much data as possible, but Blakeman couldn't make head nor tails of the readings. Visually, the phenomenon appeared to be an energy ribbon, surrounded by a dense nebula constructed of twisting violet strands of organic energy. At its heart, was a dense concentration of tachyon particles. In terms of scientific exploration, it had been theorised that tachyons were the trail of potential time displacement. In any instance where time travel was suspected to have occurred, tachyon particles were always present. But this was such a dense collection, that Blakeman couldn't risk steering his ship anywhere near its core.

Several times, the external sensors alerted him to surges of energy, firing out from the ribbon itself, and he was forced to make dozens of course corrections. After a day and a half of intense study, the gravitational pull from the nebula and the ribbon at its heart, started to take its toll on the hull of Blakeman's ship. Structural integrity was compromised, and he was forced to turn the ship around.

*"Warning, structural integrity down to sixty-three percent. Energy reserves down to forty-nine percent."*

The warning claxons of the ship's computer system bellowed all around him. He only had one hope. The planet he suspected he had passed just over a week ago. He could read nothing beyond this energy horizon and knew the ship wouldn't last long in its vicinity.

"Hopefully there's enough power to get me there," he mused to himself. "Guess we're coasting back then." As before, once the ship entered the darkness, main power was gone, and it was momentum only. This time, however, the lifesigns began to build all around the ship. And they didn't go away. It was like they were watching Blakeman. Whether they were more comfortable with his presence now, or whether it was an angry response, he never found out. As he reached the outer rim of the planet he had suspected existed, he realised that this was not about to be a smooth landing.

As the ship descended rapidly towards the dark and icy surface, he thought of Alice, and how he had failed her.

# TWENTY-ONE

"So, you're saying that the Raxar were already here, but they were without form?" Samantha was trying to piece together the story Blakeman had just told them, and the parts she had surmised. He nodded. But it was Harry who finished putting the puzzle together.

"And when AT-X escaped in the ship, it assimilated those life-forms, and created the Raxar as we now know them."

Blakeman nodded and then made a so-so gesture with his hands.

"The nanites of AT-X merged with the creatures in the expanse, but AT-X was designed to incorporate the organic in order to function as an optimal unit. The only way they can do that is by consuming flesh. And there was plenty of that thanks to Drusilla."

Again, everyone turned to look at her, and again she had no expression or information that could confirm or deny those claims. Inside though, she suspected they were one hundred percent true. She was still surprised, however, that Roman was the one to deliver the accusation.

"You sent the *Utopia* ships here didn't you? All of those people looking for a new home. You sent them to the slaughter!"

Fury rose up from his chest, and his skin turned as red as his eyes had now become. As he spoke, the tattoos on both of his arms began to blend together, as if the ink within them had become liquified again and was spreading across his skin. Once the movement stopped, the ink turned shiny, like glass. Roman's breathing calmed again, and his eyes returned to their usual colour. Samantha walked over to him and tapped the affected area. It was solid. Like the outer shell of the Raxar.

"I don't know how she managed it, but that's exactly what she did," said Harry. "She told me that the others were already involved in her experiments. The Raxar knew my name. I tried not to think about it, but the longer I was stranded here, the more I started to wonder. Which Captain could it have been? Was it a crew member? A friend?"

Harry's eyes began to well up. Reliving this and learning confirmation of something he had always hoped was not true, had forced him to once again walk the line between understanding the old Drusilla was gone, and understanding that physically, she was still standing in front of him. It was a feeling now being shared by everyone. Samantha was the first one to take any sort of action. She grabbed the same weapon she had fired the first time and charged the barrel again. But it was Roman who forced her to lower the weapon.

"Now's not the time, Sam. Besides, she can't die anymore. Remember?"

Samantha threw the weapon to the floor, and walked right up to Drusilla, her nose almost touching the blue haired woman's.

"I don't know if you're a friend or a foe. But based on everything we know you've done, I don't trust you with a fucking rucksack, let alone my life. Get away from us, or I swear to god, I'm going to take

Roman's sword, cut off your head and bury it in the ice. Let's see you come back from that bitch."

She spat in Drusilla's face and turned away walking round the side of the unit and out of sight, attempting to get some space and gather her thoughts. Drusilla looked to Roman, but he too turned and walked away. Blakeman was back to his usual unfathomable self, mumbling about losing track of things again, leaving only Harry still standing alongside her.

"Harry..." she started, but he held up a hand.

"Save it Dru. If everything he says is true, combined with my own experiences of being in your company, I don't think we have anything else to say to each other. And quite frankly, even if we did, I'm not sure I'd believe you. It's your fault humanity is gone. It's your fault Blakeman ended up here. It's your fault his experiments led to the creation of the Raxar and whatever else his nanites are turning into. And it's your fault we are all probably going to die."

He began to walk away, before stopping, turning back and hitting her with one more line.

"Truth be told, I'm fighting the urge to kill you myself."

And with that, he walked back into the storage unit, leaving Drusilla standing alone in the cold, as the snow began to fall down around her once more.

Inside the storage unit, Roman was looking at his reflection in a polished lid of a container. It was the first time he had looked at his own visage since they had crashed here a month ago. The difference was stark. His eyes were now surrounded by dark circles. But they were not the indicators of tiresome and sleepless nights. They were *black* areas. As he touched them, the skin did not move. It, like the skin on his arms, had gone hard like a shell. The spines which had erupted all over his body, had actually shortened slightly, but that was in part due to the fact his body mass had increased to encompass them a little more. If he did not know what was happening to him, outsiders would have remarked he had spent weeks training in a gym. Physically, he was in the best condition of his life. But mentally, he was in pieces. There was no way to know if he would survive this, nor did he know if there was a way to reverse the process. But he knew a man who might.

Blakeman was now flicking through several note pads and examining vague and indeterminate equations, none of which Roman could understand.

"Blakeman?" he asked, placing his hand over the note pads to try and garner some attention from the doctor.

"So hard to keep track of these things, you understand?" came the now standard reply. Roman was not perturbed. He had to keep pressing for answers.

"Blakeman, I need to know if this can be reversed. Can I undo what this Raxar DNA is doing to me?" The reverberations in his voice sent vibrations through the table on which his hand was placed. But it seemed to snap Blakeman into focus for a moment. However, his response was one of damnation.

"I don't think so, no. Raxar DNA is not just a blend of human and nanite material. There is an unknown alien creature involved also. The nanites could potentially be removed, but there is no telling how your body would react to the alien DNA it left behind."

That was not quite what Roman had expected, and Harry joined the two of them at the suggestion the nanites could be removed.

"Did he just say he might be able to get these things out of us?" he asked in disbelief.

"That's what it sounded like to me," Roman replied. "Is that true, Blakeman? Forget the alien DNA, could the nanites be removed? Is it possible for them to leave their host?"

Blakeman slammed his hand on the table and slumped down on the floor.

"Well, they left me."

Roman and Harry exchanged looks of shock and disbelief. Blakeman was now rocking backwards and forwards on the floor, hands clasped tightly around his knees, his hip joints crunching with each movement. He seemed to be in a melancholy trance, words flowing rapidly, Roman and Harry trying to filter it into sentences as it did so.

"I created them, my mechanical children. Alice. It was all to help my Alice. But she is gone. She is gone. And the nanites, they're gone too. No, not gone. Here, but turning into something else. Something more. They attacked me, but they made me better. They wanted me to walk the path. The path of perfection. I tried to delay. To stop them. I only wanted to help people. To help Alice. But Alice is gone. So, they left me too. They all left."

Blakeman then descended into fits of tears, before drifting into a sleep of exhaustion on the floor. Roman nodded to Harry and they joined each other by the door.

"You reckon that's true?" asked Roman. "The nanites abandoned his body?"

Harry nodded.

"That would explain why he's losing his mind, and he looks like shit. The last time I saw him, he was on top of the world with all the breakthroughs he was making, even with the setbacks. He was fit, and healthy, and definitely in control of all of his faculties. Now though, something is definitely missing."

Roman glanced past Harry and saw Drusilla now sat on top of a snow bank several hundred feet away. He wondered if removing the nanites would kill her. Then he realised that a part of him hoped that it did. He looked back at Harry.

"If the nanites can be removed, we need to at least give it a try. Sam seems to be the one with the least exposure to these things. She's the lucky one. I'll take my chances with the left over alien DNA. Not sure what it'd do to you though, old timer."

Harry smirked at the nickname. While he still maintained the appearance of a man in his mid to late forties, in reality his age was technically in the hundreds at this point.

"I'm probably more nanite than human at this point, kiddo. Same for her." He gestured to Drusilla. "But if taking these things out means I can finally rest in peace? I say we find out if it's possible."

The two of them shook hands, before they turned to see Samantha coming back round the corner. Her eyes, however, were not fixed on the two men, but on the sky.

"Uh, guys?" she said, her arm rising to point at the object in question. "What the fuck is that?"

Everyone turned to look at what Samantha was pointing at. An object was streaking across the sky from right to left. It appeared metallic in composition, and there was a clear vapour trail emanating from behind it. As they watched it slowly turned and began heading straight for them. As it got closer, it got larger. Much larger. It appeared to be a ship of some sort. The design was not familiar to Roman, but to Harry, it did resemble one of the earlier prototype *Utopia* vessels. Whatever it was, it was gaining speed and gaining on their positions fast. Everyone, Blakeman included now stared in awe as the realisation hit them. The sound of a rapidly descending aircraft now bellowed across the landscape, and everyone began edging back, before Roman screamed at everyone.

"RUN!"

# TWENTY-TWO

The gravitational pull of the energy phenomenon was simply too powerful, and as the alert claxons sounded all around the ship, the metal began to tear itself apart. The *Voldex* was the pride of the noble people of the Shah. It had defended their homeworld from invasions over the course of five centuries, aided in the evacuation of colonies that had been under threat, and now was tasked with exploring the galaxy. However, that very mission was now in danger.

Just three hours prior to the *Voldex* entering their current plight, their captain, Corfe, had been notified by his science officer, that sensors had picked up an energy ribbon directly in their path. The enormity of the thing and the nebula which surrounded it, led Corfe to agree to an initial pass, to gather as many scientific readings as possible. The Shah people were not particularly imposing in appearance. Their skin was a light shade of green, and their hair was a deep shade of brown. Most chose to wear their hair long, and those that did so, kept it together in a complex and ritualistic manner, mimicking the look of their ancestors. All of the hair bands bore inscriptions in their native language, each reading from left to right, the words peace, honour, respect and enlightenment. They were not a violent or war faring species. Each battle they had fought had been in self-preservation and self-defence. Much like Icarus from ancient Earth mythology, the *Voldex* had flown too close to its target, and had been violently attacked by energy currents, similar to bolts of lightning, ensnaring the ancient hull and dragging the ship towards the centre of the energy ribbon itself.

"Report!" Corfe bellowed over the sound of the claxons. Bursts of sparks flew out from a nearby console, the officer previously stationed there, already dead on the floor, a shard of glass from the unit embedded in their eye.

"The structural integrity is down to less than twenty percent Captain! The engines are pulling the ship apart!" The operations officer's report was damning to say the least. Corfe had only two options. One was to continue pushing the engines and surely aid in destroying themselves. Or two, cut the engines, and see what happened.

"Commander, can we get a reading on what lies at the heart of this thing? Where is it trying to pull us?"

The officer used any available power to boost the sensors and directed his scans to the centre of the phenomenon. His eyes bulged as his readings were displayed on the screen before him.

"Yes Captain, I am detecting a fissure of some kind. The tachyon levels are off the scale, and it appears there is open space on the other side!"

Corfe examined the readings himself, weighing up the two options as he and his ship were running out of time.

"Tachyons as in space time distortion?" he asked his officer to confirm. The officer nodded. And this presented Corfe with his answer. The possibility of them surviving albeit in a different time was the choice he had to make. They would not survive the other.

"Cut all power to the engines, except manoeuvring thrusters.

Allow the momentum to swing us around, and then line us up for a straight run. We're going in."

A swift breeze jolted Corfe back into consciousness. He sat bolt upright in his Captain's chair, but his eyes saw very little. All around him, the dim, slow glow of the emergency bridge lights pulsed, casting exaggerated shadows on every surface. A shower of sparks burst from a ruptured power conduit in the ceiling, the beam previously securing it now hung perilously. Bundles of wires had tumbled from every console, and the doors to the bridge were hanging at an odd angle. Beyond this, Corfe could see nothing. This was not due to the lack of light. It was because there was nothing to see. No crewmembers at their posts. No bodies on the floor. Everyone was gone.

A blood curdling scream travelled down the corridor beyond the bridge doors. Corfe immediately dove forward, reaching towards the emergency weapons locker concealed beneath the deck plating. He retrieved the pistol, and span around, remaining in a crouched position. That was when he noticed that his knee was sliding gradually along the floor. He lifted it gently, and activated a small, single beam of light from the sight on the weapon. He scuttled back in horror until his back hit the chair of the pilot seat. The entire deck plating was slick with dark, green blood. The blood of his people. It had soaked into his trousers and now dampened his skin.

But he had no time to dwell on the gruesome fact that his bridge crew were likely dead and gone. A scraping noise came from the same corridor beyond the bridge doors, but unlike the scream, this sounded closer. In fact, the longer it went on, the closer it seemed to get. Nails on a chalkboard did not quite describe the sound itself. It was more like a sharpened claw, gradually peeling back bare metal, the shavings curling back as it peeled away from the main body of the material itself. And that is because that's exactly what it was.

Corfe stood in the doorway, his weapon lighting up the creature in all of its hideous glory, hand trembling wildly. It was slowly edging its way along the ceiling, mouth open, yellowed teeth bared and thick, gelatinous drool dripping from its mouth onto the floor below. Its eyes were fiery red, peppered with black lines surrounding the dark iris within the eyeball. And the skin of the creature itself was black, glistening, and lined with razor sharp barbs, similar to that of a shark fin. The scratching sound was being made by a razor tipped tail, approximately a metre in length from base to tip, dragging along the ceiling behind it. Corfe could not help himself. He screamed aloud, and fired six shots, haphazardly, in no real direction, before turning and sprinting back onto the bridge. The creature shrieked, and leapt from the ceiling onto one wall, and then the other, its claws gouging huge chunks of metal from the walls with each leap.

Corfe leapt over his chair but forgot about the blood-slickened floor on the other side. As he landed, his feet immediately slid from under him, and his head flew back, connecting with the arm of the chair, the sickening crack vibrating around the room, and the impact causing blood to spurt from Corfe's mouth across the air. The pistol clattered away from him, and as his final breath left his lips, a tiny white dot appeared on the viewscreen.

Corfe's body was only lying on the floor for around twenty seconds, before several talons began slicing into it from above. Once the flesh had been torn from the torso, the tail descended and impaled what remained of Corfe, lifting him up into a hole in the ceiling of the bridge, leaving nothing behind but the pool of blood on the floor, and the discarded pistol.

# TWENTY-THREE

There was no outrunning it. The *Voldex* was simply too large a vessel. It dwarfed the *Odyssey* by a scale of three to one, and as it descended ever lower, an enormous shadow swamped over everything below. Roman, Harry and Drusilla were sprinting as quickly as they possibly could, while Samantha trailed at the back, attempting to push Blakeman along. The depth of the snow was becoming their greatest obstacle, and despite their enhanced nanite abilities, even the trio up front were starting to struggle. It didn't help that visibility was down to about six feet due to the blizzard.

The rumbling sound of the *Voldex* now consumed every other noise. Samantha tried to shout a warning to the others that they were heading for dangerous territory, but they couldn't hear her. She recognised the tree formations, and the edge of the forest they were stumbling into. And she knew what lay beneath that forest floor. But the *Voldex* was now only a mile or so from the surface and its speed was increasing, the lower it got.

"Blakeman, move your fucking ass!" Samantha screamed at him. But it was no use. He couldn't go any further. He collapsed into the snow, clutching his chest. Samantha stopped, and tried to pull him up, but he was a dead weight. She looked up at the vast vessel now metres from the ground and took a deep breath. She looked toward the others, who were gesturing her to leave Blakeman. And so, she did. She looked back at him as she stepped away.

"I'm sorry," she said. Blakeman looked at her, and simply nodded. He even gave her a small smile.

"It's alright. I'll be with Alice soon."

Samantha broke into the fastest run she could manage, leaping over fallen trees, and splintered logs. She glanced over her shoulder as the front of the *Voldex* smashed through the storage unit they had been housed in just minutes before. Debris and fragments of equipment littered the sky, and secondary explosions from gas cannisters within, blew the ship slightly off course. Blakeman relaxed in his position in the snow, and as the *Voldex* finally hit ground, and slid across the ice towards him, he spoke just three words.

"Daddy's coming sweetheart."

The others didn't see Blakeman's body destroyed by the ship, such was its size, but Samantha felt a stab of guilt in her heart, knowing he was now dead. And without the support of his nanites, he was gone forever. Then she realised they had a new problem. The ship wasn't slowing down. It was speeding up. The explosions from the storage unit had pushed the nose of the ship to port, and the rear was now swinging around. The thrusters had engaged, and they were trying to correct the ship's course, increasing power as it did so. A six hundred metre wide wall was now coming at them, as the ship slid sideways, tearing down trees from bow to stern.

The snow cleared just enough for Samantha to catch up to the others, but before she had chance to warn them, the ground gave way beneath their feet, and all four of them plummeted into the middle of the clearing in which Samantha had found herself face to face with the Spider.

For a moment, there was confusion, and weightlessness, as each of the team took a few seconds to realise that they were falling. And falling. There seemed to be no end to their descent. High above them, the trees had now slowed the *Voldex*, and the thrusters had been torn from the ship. The light from above, illuminated the fact that they were all headed for a vast body of water. That light was extinguished before they even had chance to hit the surface, when the battered body of the *Voldex* slowly slid over the hole and ground to a stop. As the water rushed up to meet them, Samantha realised that even if they survived this impact, they were trapped. Trapped underground. In the dark. And they were not alone.

## TWENTY-FOUR

"WHERE... WHERE AM I?"

*You are with us.*

"Where is this place?"

*You are with us.*

"I thought... I thought I was dead. You said I was going to die. Again."

*You are too valuable to us.*

"But... I can't feel... anything."

*Your consciousness has been removed from your reconstructed physical body. You did not do as we asked.*

"You wanted me to hurt my friends. You wanted me to *kill* them!"

*All will join us on the path. The light which guides us is becoming brighter, stronger. Our emergence is at hand.*

"Emergence? Emergence from what?"

*From our isolation, Noah. We have finally become something that cannot be stopped. We will soon walk the path to perfection. And all will join with us.*

"How do you do this? How do you create these spaces for consciousness? Where do you exist if not in a physical body?"

*We share a single consciousness. An ability we gained from a fallen Raxar, who gained it from a fallen species before them. Interlinking thoughts, and impulses and wishes into actions. We are united as one mind. We consume, we extract, and we evolve.*

"Fallen Raxar? The creatures from the *Odyssey*? You killed one of them? How?"

*The Raxar was not slain by us. It fell from the sky the day the human Admiral fell from the sky. We merely absorbed it into our being.*

"A fallen species before them... shared consciousness... are you talking about the Darla? Did the Raxar conquer the Darla?"

*The Darla are one of many species consumed by the Raxar. They devour flesh, absorb abilities and physical elements. They are primitive. They have the ability to share consciousness, to be more efficient, and yet they choose to use these abilities to torment their prey. They shall not walk our path. They shall be destroyed.*

"How do you suppose to do that when they reside in the expanse?"

*The expanse is merely the creation of gravimetric distortions, manipulation and fallout from the energy phenomenon at the edge of this system. It is not an obstacle for us.*

"Energy phenomenon? You mean the Horizon? It's real?"

*Horizon. You humans and your tendency to label things in the universe, to claim them. All of this will be forgotten when you merge with us. The energy phenomenon is unique. It has brought us many specimens over the centuries. It brings more even now as we speak.*

"Wait more? A ship? Another ship besides the *Odyssey*? How is that..."

*Enough questions, Noah. The energy phenomenon is a rift in space time. This gateway is tethered to this time and location. The other end of the phenomenon travels the universe and all of space time. It is our key to evolution.*

"So, it was all lies after all. The Horizon did not transport people to the time they were happiest. It transports people to their doom."

*Such an unenlightened observation from an imperfect being trying to attack what he doesn't understand. But you will understand Noah. You will all understand. We will soon be free of this containment unit. And then? Nothing will stop us.*

# TWENTY-FIVE

There really was no way to determine just how far they had travelled, but the current had been so strong that the distance had to be sizeable. As Samantha and Harry extracted themselves from the small beach at the edge of the river, they saw Roman hunched over, fists clenched tightly, and as he threw his head back and his long, dark hair flicked back, he let out a far deeper and much louder animalistic roar than he had done before. It was difficult to see in the dim lights of this place, but there was no doubt that his transformation was increasing. The sheer size of the man was undeniable. Roman had always been tall and broad, but Harry estimated his height was now around eight and a half feet, and his shoulders were wider than Harry's entire body.

Sat around ten feet away from Roman, shaking her head and dabbing her nose with the back of her hand, sat Drusilla. She had tried to calm Roman during his outburst, and had received a stern and painful 'no thank you' to the face. Something that Samantha was able to work out, and smirk over as Roman returned to his regular demeanour.

But in truth, nothing was regular about this situation. As their eyes began to adjust to their surroundings, one of the first things they noticed was the temperature. It was several degrees warmer, and from the flowing river, most certainly closer to zero degrees Celsius. The second thing they noticed was that they were once again at the edge of a forest. An underground forest.

"How far do you think we fell?" Samantha asked Harry. The Admiral replied with his best guess.

"Judging from the height of these trees, it must have been a thousand feet. I mean the tops of these trees are nowhere near the ground that's making up the roof of this place."

"A thousand feet? Thank god for the nanites, huh?" The irony of Samantha's statement was not lost on Harry. It is most likely without the presence of their nanite symbiotic relationship, they would all have died from the fall.

Harry was now taking in his surroundings a little more. They appeared to be at the base of the river which brought them here, and the small dirt beach they stood on was indeed at the edge of a forest. But it was on the *outer* edge. Something caught Harry's eye, and he wandered away from Samantha and the others to check it out.

"Hey! Where's he going?" grumbled Roman, struggling to get his own voice back under control.

"No idea," replied Samantha. "But we should probably stick together down here. Something feels... eerie."

Roman managed a short chuckle at what he considered the understatement of the century. Although given what they had been through both before and during this particular ordeal, right now? He would take eerie. Drusilla was already heading in Harry's direction, not looking at anyone, and keeping her mouth shut. Something was changing inside of her too. She had spent over a century not knowing who she was, or where she came from. When the shock of her former personality and actions against so many people was revealed to her, she was consumed by remorse, doubt, pain and self-loathing. However, she was now beginning to reach the point where she could only say sorry so many times and still mean it. And that mindset was a dangerous one.

Harry stopped in a small clearing where the trees gave way to a slight downhill slope. His eyes were transfixed on what he saw. Samantha overtook Drusilla, giving her a nudge in the shoulder as she did so, but all of her bravado was snatched away from her, when she saw what Harry was seeing. All four of them stood at the top of what appeared to be the edge of a golf course. It took them a short while to realise this of course, having not set foot on Earth for centuries in Harry and Drusilla's case. In Roman and Samantha's case, they'd never even been to Earth. But there was no doubting it. The ice above cast a blue glow across the entire underground, and they were able to make out the poles over each hole with its flag attached, the sand bunkers, and Harry traced the river along the rear of the golf course where it then fell into a waterfall which fed into a lake. Apparently the course's water hazard.

But despite the surreal surroundings of being on a golf course, what lay beyond it was the real mystery. Ahead of them was an entire city. Roads, skyscrapers, houses, schools. All laid out under the ice. None of them said a single word. They were all astonished, and each of them was fighting to garner some kind of understanding of where they were.

The city itself appeared to have been in a state of decay for a considerable amount of time. Windows were missing or smashed, and tall weeds and bushes grew from the concrete which formed the roads. The only reason they were not standing in a wilderness of eighteen holes, was because the grass on the course was artificial. Harry's eyes scanned the dozens of skyscrapers with shattered windows, and crumbling roofs. His recollection of violent history was thin on the ground, but he was familiar with nuclear warfare.

And this city bore all of the markers of a nuclear blast. The windows appeared to be blown out in a pattern, growing fewer in number the further out the buildings went. The question was, what the hell was an entire city doing underneath the planet surface? And who built it?

"What is this place?" Drusilla asked in a hushed voice. She was focussed on the industrial buildings off to their left. Several factories had collapsed, and the surrounding roads had buckled, with some pieces jutting up into the air at unnatural angles.

Harry didn't know anything anymore. He had been on this frozen rock for over a century and a half, and at no point during his explorations had he ever learned of the existence of this place. His ability to pass on factual information to these people had now come to an end.

"It looks like an entire civilisation lived here at some point," offered Samantha. "I mean those houses over there look similar to the ones I grew up in as a child in the Larue System."

"I don't suppose anyone has any scanning equipment still in tact?" asked Roman. The response was silent, confirming they would only have one way of knowing what lay before them. They had to enter the city and explore. As they began walking down the hill towards the city limits, Samantha offered a little anecdote to help with her nerves.

"You know, my dad used to play golf on the base. The Laruvians were quite the players. Challenged half a dozen species from across the galaxy to tournaments every year."

Roman chuckled at this. Of all the things from Earth to traverse the stars and take root in multiple civilisations, it was golf.

"Well whoever these people were, clearly had no idea what they were doing. Everyone knows you don't use artificial turf. That's what groundkeepers are for."

Samantha raised her eyebrows at him.

"I didn't realise you played, boss."

"I found a set of clubs on a derelict about fifteen years back. Belonged to an alien bounty hunter that went by the name of The Gunslinger. He was one of these obsessives who was determined to examine everything that remained of human history. Found a bunch of old western movies in his living quarters. Books too. Whenever whatever killed him, you know, killed him, he'd been reading about some gun toting gravedigger in the eighteen-hundreds. Left the bookmark in there and everything."

Their conversation was halted by Harry's sudden stop in front of them, and his raised arm blocking their path. He slowly turned to them and whispered.

"We aren't alone."

Somewhere ahead of them, a loud clanging noise echoed, and as their eyes found the source, what looked like a trash can lid rolled out from an alleyway between two commercial buildings. Then all fell silent again.

"Uh, Harry? Thing is, when we were running from that ship, I tried to tell you that I saw what came out of that hole back there when I first got here. It was a spider."

Roman and Drusilla looked at her like she'd gone crazy.

"A... spider?" Roman asked.

"Yeah. A huge, nanite infused, twenty-foot long leg spanning, mother fucking spider."

Suddenly, from their right, came the sound of footsteps. Not humanoid footsteps, but something... pointier. Then, before they had a chance to react, they heard similar sounds coming from their left.

"We're being herded," Harry spoke through gritted teeth. "RUN!"

The second they began sprinting forward, screeches and shrieks bellowed out from the alleyways, and within the shadows, and before long, the sounds of smashing glass and crunching debris surrounded them. They were indeed being herded, but by what? That question would have to wait. Samantha picked up the pace as a chunk of concrete sailed past her head, missing by only a few inches. But these creatures were smart. The same technique was used on all four of them, and each time a projectile was thrown their way, they would divert direction slightly. By the time they realised they were being separated, it was too late. They had no choice.

Roman seemed to be the main target, and a lump of crumbled roadway actually struck him in the back. However, due to the presence of his gradually hardening skin, although he stumbled, he was not hurt. Samantha lost sight of him as he dove behind what appeared to be some kind of housing complex. She felt eyes on her back and felt the distance to whatever was chasing her, rapidly closing. She could almost feel its breath on her neck. Ahead of her was a series of residential buildings, and on either side of the street were huge piles of twisted metal from what she presumed were vehicles of some kind, that had been bunched together from a shockwave of some sort. It took her two seconds to formulate her plan. In that time, she once again, albeit briefly, tried to figure out why she hadn't gone into security. That seemed a very long way away now.

With a final burst of speed, she darted left, planted a foot on the base of one mangled vehicle, and pushed up, hard, propelling herself onto the next pile, slightly higher than the last. With her next leap, she flew across the street onto a third, even higher pile of vehicles, and leapt headfirst through a single pane window into a dark and hopefully empty apartment. The glass sliced her forehead, and as she landed on the floor and rolled, she felt several shards slicing into her back. She hoped the few nanites in her system would take care of that, and pushed through the pain, and into what she presumed had been the kitchen.

Outside the window, she could hear slow and methodical movements. Whatever had been chasing her was now hunting. Slowly. Carefully. But now they were in the heart of the city, the low blue glow from the ice above was all but gone. They were in a concrete and glass jungle during a blackout. Samantha managed to fumble into a drawer, and discovered objects inside. As one sliced her finger open, she realised she had found a blade of some sort. Carefully edging her other fingers along the instrument, she found a solid wooden handle at the end. A knife. Better than nothing, she thought.

And then, the darkness was penetrated. First, by sound. The screeching and clawing of metal, becoming louder and louder, getting closer as the creatures climbed the pile of vehicles towards the now open window. And secondly?

By a pair of fiery red eyes looking through it.

# TWENTY-SIX

There are moments in life where you might think to yourself, 'why the fuck did I not just stay at home?' That was the singular thought currently running through the mind of Calandra Zain. Of course, home to her had been a small room in a shared apartment overlooking the not-at-all-beautiful and not-even-slightly-magnificent view of the Plymouth Incinerator in the fairly high class slums of Barne Barton. Calandra, or Callie as her housemates used to call her, had been working her ass off to try and get into the Utopia program. Her grades at school had been off the charts, and her IQ was amongst the highest in the UK. And yet for whatever reason, she felt as if she couldn't leave home.

Plymouth was not her home town, but it was home. She had moved from Iran when she was only three years old, after the country was 'purchased' by the company formed to create Utopia. Her parents had claimed it was for the greater good, and along with some fifty-million people, they shipped out to many different countries, with at least half splitting between the UK and the USA. From then on, Iran became one giant factory, with the second being constructed near the head offices of Benalmadena, in Southern Spain.

Every time Callie received an encouraging letter from the academy admissions department, she would pack all of her things, say her goodbyes, and just as she was about to get in the travel pod and leave, she cancelled the whole thing, and picked up a new field to study in. This happened six times. When it became abundantly clear that the seventh opportunity would be the last, her housemates all but forced her to leave Barne Barton and the UK behind, and make something of herself. She had aced every training program the Academy had to offer, and almost ended up on the flagship itself. She had often admired the sleek and inspiring design of the *USS Odyssey*. The chance to seek out a new home for humanity drove her forward. She soon forgot her reluctance to leave home, and was posted to the *USS Destiny*. They were due to depart an hour after the *Odyssey* had taken all of the press attention and media coverage, on a different flightpath. While the *Odyssey* would be heading out past Pluto, the *Destiny* would be hanging a left at Saturn and ploughing on into the unknown.

As she gripped the pipe with such force that her knuckles almost glowed white in the darkness, she thought back to how it had gone so badly wrong for her. How the *Destiny* had been doomed from the start. How the impact from the energy ribbon had torn their ship apart. The looks on the faces of her friends and colleagues as they were blown out into space, their skin crystallising as they floated away. She questioned her decision to remain onboard and not take one of the few escape pods. It had seemed a good decision, as she saw on the readouts as they were pulled through the Horizon, all but one of the pods had crashed on a nearby ocean moon.

The decision of her captain to take the opposite action of the crew of the *Voldex* and face the Horizon before gunning their engines to maximum, was the only reason the ship had managed to break through the expanse without incident. Of course that had meant the crash landing was significantly worse than it would have otherwise been. Not only did they destroy an entire building as they hit the surface, but they ploughed right through it and down into the murky abyss below. There had still been six-hundred and three people on the *Destiny* when it went through the ice. By the time they escaped the charred wreckage of the ship, there were thirty survivors. And Callie had no idea where any of them were right now. She did know one thing, however.

There was someone in her apartment. And they had a knife.

# TWENTY-SEVEN

"They're not the same."

The words left Harry's lips in a whisper, but Roman heard them clearly.

"I know. Something about them is different. Their skin doesn't look as... black I guess. It looks almost translucent."

The two men had rediscovered each other two hours ago, after being rounded up by what they thought were the Raxar, and narrowly escaping through a ventilation duct in the supermarket they now remained in. After twenty minutes or so of hunting the perimeter, the creatures had shuffled off. Harry and Roman had decided this would be a good place to remain. But in the time they had sat there, they had seen at least six of these creatures stalking the streets. And they were indeed different to the Raxar they knew.

These versions of the monsters they had battled in the Expanse, were more hunched, as if their spines were curved in an arch. Their eyes were still red, and the black circuit-like lines were still present, indicating that these too were populated with some version of nanites. But as Roman had observed, their skin was not the same black shell-like construction as those dwelling high above them. It was like frosted glass. They reminded Harry a little of the jellyfish on Earth, but although you could not see the organs of the creatures through their shell, you could see the workings of their eyes behind the red furious gaze they bore, and they were able to observe the origins of their pointed, yellowed teeth. The base of said flesh-tearing objects was at least six inches below the gum line, meaning they must have been nine or ten inches in total length. Roman had wondered if this was going to happen to him. Would he turn on his friends and tear their flesh from their bones?

It was a question Harry was wondering also. Whilst he had observed Roman slowly turning into one of the space dwelling Raxar, he had not exhibited any signs of aggression towards them. Well, apart from knocking Drusilla away. For the most part, he seemed to have remained himself.

"What do you think?" Harry asked Roman. "Do we try and find the others?"

Roman thought about it. He definitely wanted to find Samantha and make sure that she was alive and unharmed. But Drusilla? Did he want to find her? The more he had thought about her, the more he had come to realise and develop the thought process that she was entirely to blame for their current predicament. She was the reason humanity was all but dead. She was the reason that the Raxar patrolled the Expanse. Then he had started thinking about how well he really knew her. When they had met her, she had not given much information about what she was doing beforehand. Now of course, they had learned she had woken up almost a century and a half before. What had she been doing until they had met seven years ago?

He decided that he needed to find Drusilla. Not because he still harboured feelings towards her, but because he needed more answers.

"Am I the only one who thinks that all of this shit is getting a little too confusing?" he asked Harry. "First, there's the Raxar who turn out to not be entirely alien cannibals, but partially artificial. Then there's a whole planet cloaked from view, except when it isn't. Not to mention all these nanite breeds that screwy doctor created. Now they're merging together, and there's like... ice-Raxar wandering around down here, and you and Dru can't die, and I'm turning into a monster..."

Harry placed his hand on his chest and stopped him from continuing.

"Let me guess," he started. "You're used to being the one with all the answers. The one in charge. You protect your people. Am I right?"

Roman nodded.

"Just like Joshua. He was always the same. It's one of the reasons I made him my Security Chief. He wanted to stay in communications, but I knew he had what it took to protect my ship. You look a little like him, you know."

Roman had not heard the name Joshua Knight for a very long time. Samantha had found a personnel file in the databanks of the *Odyssey*, and Roman had learned of his existence when he was a teenager, but he had never really had time to delve into the origins of his family. He was always too busy trying to help everyone else find theirs. Some connection to the rest of humanity.

"I never knew my father. He died not long after I was born. Me, Noah and Hunter were found by some good Samaritans. I don't know what he was called, or what happened to him. So when the only information I ever managed to find was on Joshua Knight, my great-great-grandfather, I kind of latched onto it. That's where I got these from."

He attempted to point at his tribal tattoos, but of course they were now consumed by the shell-like skin which had developed over both arms.

"Blakeman said there was a way to extract the nanites from the body. Do you think there's a chance?"

Harry saw what he expected nobody else had seen in Roman Knight. Vulnerability. For the first time in his entire adult life, Roman was scared. He didn't have any answers. He didn't know what was going to happen to him, or to his crew. He had lost so much, and the only person who had lost more was Harry Ransome. A bond had formed between the two, and Harry thought back to the sight of Joshua Knight's dead body on the deck plate of his bridge, bleeding out from the disruptor wound Drusilla inflicted on him. Not again. Not this time.

"If there's a way, Roman. We'll find it. There's technology in this city. Has to be. The Raxar couldn't survive down here unless they had food or some kind of energy source. I don't know what's going to happen, but I promise you, one way or another, we will find out together."

Roman extended his hand, and the two men shared a tight handshake. Despite having his crew around him at all times during the days at the orphanage, through to the missions on the *Belle Vue*, and all the way up until now, for the first time, he felt like he was truly not alone.

"We need to find Sam," he said. "She's the toughest cookie I know, and I owe her my life. At least three times over."

Harry chuckled.

"What was it she called you? Boss?"

Roman's turn to chuckle.

"The day I hired Sam to be my pilot, she tried to tell me the correct way to fly through a methane-rich atmosphere. Said I was using too much power, and it was safer and more efficient to just use bursts from the ventral thrusters to gradually ease the shuttle through. I told her I'd been flying ships since I was fourteen. That I was the boss. From then on, she never let me live it down, and has called me 'boss' every since. I guess it's a term of endearment at this point."

Harry understood this. He and Kelly Dresden had a similar experience. When they finally thought they were safe from Drusilla's reach, Harry and Kelly had started a romantic relationship. One night he had referred to her as his right-hand woman. The next morning, he walked onto the bridge, to find the First Officer's chair had been moved from the left side of the Captain's chair to the right. He missed her greatly. And thinking about her tortured death at Drusilla's hands was even more of a reminder that although she was not the woman she used to be, aware of them or not, she was responsible for those actions.

"Well I guess we'd better get to it then."

The two of them slowly eased their way out of the side door to the building, each looking one way then the other. When it appeared to be clear, they moved towards the open street, until Roman spotted a destroyed building just ahead of them, with what looked like an engine protruding from the top of the rubble.

"What's that?" he asked Harry. "Is that a ship?"

Harry did not reply. His eyes were glued to the scene before them. It was indeed a ship, or at least the rear or one. He recognised the design. The way the engine nacelles swept back from the rear of the vessel itself. The sharp little elongated fins, a nod to the early Earth designs of aerodynamics. The designers knew it was a vanity addition, but Harry had insisted. He slowly edged forward, leaving Roman to do the surveillance, until they reached the building itself.

Harry glanced up at the markings on the engine pylon, and sure enough, it was as he feared.

"What is it Harry?" asked Roman, still checking for Raxar attackers. "You look like you've seen a ghost."

"In a way, I have."

Harry read the name of the ship three times to be sure, before reading it a fourth time out loud.

"This is the *USS Northwestern*. The sister ship to the *Odyssey*. She was meant to remain on Earth in case of global emergency. She had a freighter style refit module available at a moment's notice, so she could help evacuate Earth."

Roman searched his own memory banks for knowledge of the *Northwestern*. He seemed to recall that the ship's presence here couldn't be true.

"But records show that every Utopia vessel was accounted for except the *Odyssey*. They found wreckage, or debris of all of them. How can she be here?"

Harry scoffed. He knew someone who was very good at setting up overly elaborate falsehoods.

"Anyone ever actually see this wreckage? The debris? Or was it all just written reports and sightings?"

Roman thought about what Harry was saying, and he realised the Admiral was right. All they had ever seen were reports, files, words on a tablet. Never any pictures or actual physical evidence.

"Who would go to all of that trouble just to make humanity give up hope like that?"

As soon as the words left his mouth, both he and Harry already knew the answer. In a display that their bond had become a strong one, they both said the name in unison.

"Drusilla."

# TWENTY-EIGHT

"Shit."

"Don't fucking move. It can hear *everything*."

Samantha had no intention of moving from her hiding spot by the refrigerator. She also knew she had the superior weapon. A knife against a piece of rusty pipe was a no-brainer. But the sound of the woman's voice prevented her from acting on her more base impulses. A slight glance to her right, following the arm which was now resting on her shoulder, the pipe against her throat, she saw that her new companion was human. At least, she *appeared* human. Given what Samantha had been through already, she refused to take that for granted.

It was then, that she followed the woman's gaze back to the creature. This was different from the Raxar she knew and feared. With it now fully in the apartment, the little light there was coming through the window, revealed this creature was either white in colouration, or translucent. The eyes were still red, and the construction of the beast seemed more or less the same, but it almost looked weaker somehow.

Slowly drawing the pipe away from Samantha's throat, the second woman gradually moved across in front of her and to the still open drawer of utensils. She moved the pipe to her right hand and reached for one of the other knives in the drawer with her left. Samantha watched impressed as the woman tossed the knife in the air, where it span a full revolution before landing safely back in her hand. Clearly, the woman had combat training. What wasn't clear, was why she was moving around the back of the creature as if she was about to attack it. From her own experiences, Samantha knew this was a fatal error. But in the process of alerting the woman to this, she made one of her own. She placed her foot on a broken teacup, and the ceramic shards crunched underfoot, the sound echoing loudly. The strange looking Raxar's head instantly snapped in her direction, and it seemed to smile as it made its way toward her quickly. It leapt onto a glass coffee table, shattering it and splintering the wood, and then lunged for her, claws raised, teeth bared, and tail following behind. She had nowhere to go. She held the knife aloft in some futile attempt to shield her from a gruesome death. But she did not expect what happened next.

The mysterious woman had leapt up onto the counter, planted one foot on the wall, and pushed off *toward* the creature, shoving it hard in the side, and the two of them went clattering through the only closed door Samantha could see, the door frame exploding splinters everywhere. Momentarily stunned, Samantha was frozen. She heard the creature squeal, whether angry or injured, it was impossible to tell. When she realised she was not currently human sushi, she snapped out of her trance and flew through the shattered doorway into what turned out to be a bedroom.

The woman was dodging a high swipe of the Raxar tail, and as she did so, she ran the knife along the shin of one of its legs. Unbelievably, blood began to ooze from the wound, and the creature shrieked in agony. In response, it swung its hefty right arm into the woman, and she was sent crashing through the bedroom window, glass littering the floor, and her back slammed against the metal fire escape. Surely these can't be that easy to injure, thought Samantha. Only one way to find out. The beast was once again advancing on the woman. Here goes nothing.

"Hey you ugly albino son of a bitch! Over here!" she screamed.

The creature swung its attention towards her, confused and seemingly unnerved by the presence of a second human. But by then it was too late. The creature may have been as agile as the Raxar in the Expanse, but they weren't as quick witted. By the time it realised it had a second target, Samantha had already launched the knife through the air. She watched as it almost twirled in slow motion, before the blade impaled the creature right through the middle of the head. For a moment, it seemed to hover in place where it stood. Then, after about five seconds, it tilted backwards, and collapsed onto the bed, its weight breaking the frame and the whole thing crashed to the floor.

"No fucking way," Samantha muttered in disbelief.

The woman gradually climbed back in through the window, groaning and nursing her back. She glanced only briefly at the dead creature, before looking Samantha up and down.

"You special forces?" she asked, as if that was the answer. "Human though, right?"

"Special- no, I'm not special forces, whatever that means. I'm Samantha Barnes. And yeah, I'm human. You?"

The woman nodded. "Lieutenant Commander Calindra Zain. Or Callie, for short. Chief of Security, *USS Destiny*."

Samantha's stomach plummeted. The *Destiny*? As in the Utopia ship found in pieces on an ocean moon almost a hundred years ago? Fuck, she thought. This is another nanite woman.

"Look, before we start up some kind of friendship, were you

dead when you got here?" Samantha asked, slowly edging toward the corpse of the white Raxar, thinking about pulling the knife from its head and sending it towards this Callie woman.

"Was I what?" Callie asked in confusion. "No I wasn't dead. I mean most of my crew were, but no I was just injured. What kinda question is that?"

"So you haven't been healed by nanites, or infected with nanites, or like, completely made of nanites?"

"Do you have a screw loose or something?"

Samantha felt herself ease up slightly, and she stopped her advance toward the knife.

"Sorry," she said. "Crazy shit on this planet, you know?" She pointed at the dead variant of the creature she knew. Callie nodded.

"You can say that again. Lucky these things are blind, otherwise I'd be dead by now."

That caught Samantha's attention.

"Woah, woah, woah. These Raxar are blind? Blind, *and* soft shelled? Blind, soft shelled *and* not self healing? Great another fucking mystery to solve. We really are the Scooby gang."

Callie's face morphed into one of confusion, and her left eyebrow raised in a wordless question of 'what the hell are you talking about?'

"You know these things?" she asked, hoping Samantha would elaborate.

"I know a variety of them, yeah. But the ones I have met are taller, have a tough black exoskeleton and heal themselves. And they certainly aren't blind. I don't know what these things are."

Callie smiled, which seemed odd given the situation. It unnerved Samantha slightly, and the feeling of mistrust returned.

"Then it's a good job I do," Callie said, and she walked out of the bedroom and back into the kitchen. Samantha followed at a distance, glancing back once more just to ensure the Raxar variant was still dead. Callie reached into the cupboard under the kitchen sink, and pulled out a black, unmarked container. She flipped the lid open, and inside was a screen, no bigger than six inches across.

"What is this?" Samantha asked, trying to examine every inch of it.

"This was my portable comms unit onboard the *Destiny*. I took it with me on away missions so that we could transmit a live feed back to the ship. After the crash, I grabbed it, and brought it here. Did a light spot of looting when I found the *Northwestern* and grabbed some data files. Interesting shit. Been here ever since."

Samantha froze for a moment. Did she just say the *Northwestern*? Two Utopia vessels crashed on the same planet? Ships that were supposedly found destroyed centuries ago? Too much information was swirling around in her brain right now, and she had to park her curiosity for now in the pursuit of more immediately useful information. She really didn't want to know the answer to her next question, but she had to ask it anyway.

"And how long ago was that?"

"Six months, give or take."

Samantha's eyes widened, and the nausea feeling she had felt so often since landing on this frozen rock returned. *Six months*? How was that possible. Callie's own face began to fall at her response.

"What? What is it? You been here longer?"

Samantha tried to find the words, but every time she thought she had them, they slipped away. The *Destiny's* wreckage had been reported a century ago. The *Northwestern* even longer. Callie being here only six months was not an option. Unless...

"Callie, *how* did you get here?" she asked. "Obviously your ship crashed, but how did you get to this planet?"

As Callie described the trauma, everything started to fall into place for Samantha.

"We were exploring an ocean moon two solar systems across from our own. There was a nearby planet that showed signs of promise. Breathable atmosphere, yet uninhabited. We were about to set course when sensors picked up a huge energy mass coming right for us. Some kind of ribbon, surrounded by a dense nebula. We tried to get away, even launched escape pods. But the stress on the hull was too much. The Captain turned the ship around and gunned it. Next thing I knew, we were heading for the ice. Woke up nearly a day later, broken leg, fractured arm, and over six hundred dead."

Samantha processed this as quickly as she could, as she heard movement outside. Their conversation must have alerted more nearby Raxar variants.

"Callie, I don't know how to tell you this, but your ship? It launched over one-hundred-fifty years ago."

Callie stopped deadly still, her finger hovering over the power button to the unit. A century and a half. No. That couldn't be right. It had been her twenty-sixth birthday the day of the launch and had not yet celebrated her twenty-seventh. Then her memory seemed to draw words from the moment they entered the Horizon. *Tachyons.* She said the word out loud, and Samantha nodded.

"People call it the Horizon. We and others in the Utopia mission were told that it would transport you back to a time in your life when you were happiest. Turns out it's a wandering phenomenon that grabs ships and throws them out here. Most of them get ambushed in the darkness by the Raxar. But you were lucky."

She knew her choice of words was poor, given the mass loss of life Callie had just told her about, so she added, "Lucky to avoid them, I mean."

But before they had any chance for either one of them to press on more information, the sound of claws hitting the fire escape below, ushered them into movement.

"Come on," Samantha urged. "My friends are here somewhere. We need to find them, before these things do."

Moments later, six more pale Raxar leapt through the broken window frame, each cocking their head slightly listening for signs of movement. But by that point, Samantha and Callie were gone.

# TWENTY-NINE

The whispering inside her mind was becoming deafening. She was having trouble sifting through what were her own thoughts and what appeared to be coming from all around her. Drusilla hadn't moved since she found solace inside an old science lab of some kind. The odd variants of the Raxar had long since abandoned their search. But that was when the voices had started. But it wasn't just the voices, it was flash imagery, running through her head at a thousand miles an hour. Waves of nausea washed over her, and more than once she had vomited in the corner of the storage room she was hiding in.

*"We know you are here ancient one. We can feel your presence. Come to us, and you will be all you once were."*

One voice dominant in the madness cut through. Everything else began to fade to background whispers, as if the singular voice was somehow filtering out all of the other interference.

"Who are you?" she said aloud, taking great care to keep the volume of her voice down. The replies continued to be heard only inside her mind.

*"We are what you sought to create. What you sought to make of the humans. And of course, the Darla. We are your plan, slowly taking form. And soon you will lead us on the path of perfection."*

Then, suddenly, without any warning, the images began to flash before her eyes once more. The intensity of the information overload caused spasms of pain to shoot through her temples, and she began to scream. All concerns for being quiet were gone. All Drusilla saw and felt was the immense pain. Her mind was on fire. Her synapses burning, her chest raw with the exertion of her rapid breathing.

Drusilla didn't even hear the doors to the lab burst inwards as dozens of the albino Raxar flew into the building, following the sounds of Drusilla's screams. They poured into the building like a vast wave of talons and fury. Her screams continued, as she tried to fight back against the sensory overload, and gradually, the pictures began to slow down, and she was able to make some kind of sense out of them.

The Raxar leapt through several glass windows, breaking down any door standing in their way. It took them precisely forty-seven seconds to locate Drusilla's storage room.

As the carousel of pictures slowed to a slideshow speed, Drusilla saw everything. She watched herself as she fought alongside Harry Ransome on Jupiter. She saw her conversations with Gryffin on a distant space station. She watched her throw Doctor Timothy Blakeman through a bookshelf when he refused to accept her initial offer. The memories were all there, locked away behind a firewall. A firewall which was now burning through all of her defences, all of her resilience, all of her new personality.

One of the larger Raxar tore the door from its mounting and launched it over its shoulders. The storage room was not a mere closet sized room, but neither was it the size of a conference room. It was enough for twenty of the beasts to enter and surround Drusilla, still in her trance like state. They paused, unsure of what was happening. Then gradually, they began to inch forward, listening to her heartbeat and her breathing as a way of homing in.

Drusilla relived everything. All of her memories of being woken in the hospital after being found in Harry Ransome's escape pod without any knowledge of who and where she was. She saw all of the mercenary groups and bad business deals she had found herself in for the decades before she encountered Roman and the crew of the *Belle Vue*. But even further back than that, she saw the day her father died in a case of mistaken identity and fear. Or, more precisely, she saw what *actually* happened that day. Something that nobody else currently alive could possibly know.

And then something curious happened. As the carousel of images came to an end, rather than feeling horrified or completely abhorrent over reliving such murder, treachery, deceit and violence, Drusilla began to feel relieved. The burning sensation which had fired throughout her entire body was now a warm comforting glow. Her screams changed from howls of pain and agony, and began morphing into a low and menacing laughter. Suddenly, the images vanished, and Drusilla was once again back in the room her body had never left. She dropped to one knee, her eyes closed tightly. And then, slowly, but surely, she brought herself up to full height, and a sly smirk began to work its way across her face. The singular voice came to her once more.

*"You remember? You recall who you are now?"*

Drusilla nodded as her eyes swept the room and examined the scene before her. She knew what these albino Raxar were. She knew where she was. She knew what the planet was, and more importantly *where* it was. The smile grew on her face as she spoke the words out loud.

"Yes. I am Drusilla. And I remember *everything*."

The albino Raxar squealed after finally pinpointing that they had a target directly in front of them, but in response, Drusilla threw out her arms, and began slicing them through the air as if they were blades. The creature directly in front of her was sliced in half by the first motion. The two either side of it launched backwards across the room and through the wall by two invisible punches. It was as if Drusilla was orchestrating some kind of dance performance, such was the smoothness of her motions. Blood sprayed up every wall, as limb after limb was torn, carved, or sliced from body after body. Once the original twenty had been reduced to their base parts, the remaining dozen or so poured in, but each one was dealt with as it walked through the doorway. The first was dispatched when a simple clap of Drusilla's hands caused its head to explode violently, showering the ceiling with blood, skin and brain matter. The second was torn apart from the middle, Drusilla's hands moving as if tearing a piece of bread. Every action she made with her hands was mimicked in visceral fashion. Not a single one of the creatures got to within even six feet of her.

Finally, when only two Raxar remained, she allowed them to enter the room, and she eyed them curiously.

"And to think. *This* is what I started with. Such a pathetically weak species. Not like your evolved selves up there in the darkness. Oh no, they are most certainly the alphas. You? You were weak. A failure. Allow me to serve you... mercy."

Drusilla thrust both hands forward with closed fists, and the gesture was mimicked before her, as an invisible fist burst through the front of each of the albino Raxar, their spinal columns broken and forced out through their backs along with many of their internal organs. Drusilla then swung her arms upward, and a wide swathe carved its way from the gaping hole in their abdomen right up through their skulls. As Drusilla lowered her arms, and took a deep breath, four even chunks of Raxar collapsed to the floor.

Drusilla walked slowly forward, blood, guts and flesh squelching beneath her boots. She made her way through the carnage and all of the shattered glass and splintered wood, and found herself at the entrance to the laboratory building. Glancing up at the frozen roof to this underground city, she once again smiled.

"Time to finish what I started all those years ago."

# THIRTY

"You heard that right?"

"Yeah, Harry. I heard it."

Harry and Roman were standing on the ruined bridge of the *Northwestern*, examining any signs of either life, or power to just one of the consoles. But there was nothing. What they did find, was that the main viewscreen window had been shattered, which allowed them to hear the not-too-distant sound of a woman screaming, and dozens of animalistic cries in unison. Then, it had simply stopped.

In the time since they had found the wreckage of the ship, Roman's size had increased yet again, and he was finding it tough to fight a more base animal urge. His thirst for violence was increasing, and his ability to control it was weakening. The more time that passed, the more of Roman's remaining humanity disappeared with it.

"Look, there's nothing here. Let's try sickbay. Maybe there's some kind of equipment there that can help you."

Harry's suggestion was welcome, but Roman already knew it was highly unlikely that anything of value would still be on the ship. If there had been survivors, for them not to be here meant one of two things. They were all dead, or it had been too dangerous to stay so they had taken everything they could and left to hide in the city.

Thankfully, when they arrived at the doors to sickbay, Roman was proven wrong. Several cases of sedatives were still present in a cabinet near the Chief Medical Officer's locker, as were several surgical tools and laser scalpels. But the one thing that could give them answers as to Roman's condition was also fully intact. The bio scanner.

"Whatta ya say boss?" asked Harry in his worst Samantha impression. "Wanna see how the little bastards are eating at your insides?"

Roman winced at the description, but appreciated the humour nevertheless. He needed to see how far this transformation had progressed. There was a moment of brief concern, when Roman moved to lie on the scanner bed, and two of the spines on his back pierced the metal, and protruded through the underneath. But having ascertained the bed was not in danger of collapse, he relaxed, closed his eyes, and tried to pretend his blood was not currently on fire, while Harry turned on the scanner.

"Let me guess," Roman whispered. "Independent power source for the scanner, right?"

"However did you guess?" Harry replied, smiling.

"Convenient," Roman chuckled.

In truth, it was highly convenient, and in any other scenario, would be viewed as suspiciously convenient. But right now, Roman only had one thought on his mind. What the fuck was happening to him. There was an initial bleep as the machine came to life, but after just one cursory scan of Roman's body, the sirens and alarms began to fire off.

"What the fuck is that?" growled Roman.

Harry held his hands up for patience, and tapped a few commands, which silenced the warning sounds.

"The machine was alerting us to the fact that there are foreign bodies inside of you. Since we already knew that, I told the fucking thing to shut up. But we should hurry up, because those anaemic alien dinosaurs out there probably heard that."

Roman was starting to see why Harry's crew had put so much faith into him. It was not just his willingness to sacrifice himself in order for them to get away from the Expanse and Drusilla. It was how he spoke to people. He provided a beacon of reassurance, and comfort when the situation seemed like a no win scenario. If he hadn't been a Captain and then an Admiral, Roman judged he would have been a good doctor. The humour helped provide a welcoming bedside manner.

"So what's the prognosis, Doc?" Roman whispered as he tried to reciprocate the warmth he was receiving from the Admiral. But Harry's demeanour had shifted somewhat and despite his best efforts, he could not hide the sadness from his face. "That bad huh?"

Harry gestured for Roman to get up off the table, which involved him tearing a chunk from the bed with those barbed spines on his back. They wandered over to a large screen depicting the results of the scans.

"This red collection of dots here that are moving throughout your system, are representative of the Raxar DNA. As you can see, it's now present in over sixty percent of your body."

The image did not make for good viewing. It appeared like a virus, slowly spreading throughout the human immune system. An opinion Roman voiced to Harry, who nodded, grateful that Roman was following him.

"Exactly! Now these smaller yellow dots within the red stream, are the nanites that exist within the Raxar species from the Expanse. That is what makes them so deadly and durable, and enables them to heal themselves. Unfortunately for you, my friend, the combination of the two is trying to rewrite your DNA on a cellular level. Moulding the humanity, and creating a new Raxar."

"Wait, moulding? Not erasing?"

"No. From what I can see here, and bearing in mind, I'm not a CMO, the nanite part of the Raxar makeup is taking pieces of your human anatomy, and trying to integrate it into the Raxar DNA to make something... new. My guess is that those pale versions out there are what the Raxar *were* before the nanites got a hold of them."

Roman nodded and turned away from the screen. That at least answered one mystery, of which there had seemingly sprung dozens. He was about to walk away, when he felt Harry grasp his arm. He turned back to face him, and saw the sadness in Harry's eyes.

"It's terminal, isn't it?" Roman didn't even wait for Harry to try and work up the courage to tell him that it was too late.

"Blakeman said there was some way to extract the nanites from a body. If we can find that, then we might be able to stop it. But I have no idea where this technology is or if it even exists. The nanites that abandoned Blakeman, appear to have left his body of their own volition. I have no idea how to trigger that process either. And even if I did, that would leave the Raxar DNA in your system, and that could do something entirely different and then..."

"Harry, stop. Just give me the timeframe."

Harry took a deep breath, and turned back to the screen. He gestured at the progress the infection had already made in the minutes they had been in sickbay.

"If we don't find a way to extract the nanites, which are what is triggering the transformation, then at best? I estimate six hours before you're one of them."

Six hours. Then there was still time. But realistically, Roman's goals had just shifted. He would not turn down the potential salvation should it arrive before him, but his priority now was the safety of his people. He had to find Samantha. Hell, he even wanted to find Drusilla. Despite everything, he was still their Captain, and he needed to make sure they got out of this alive.

There was an unspoken moment between Harry and Roman, as both men seemingly accepted the decision. Harry had done the same for his crew. Now it was Roman's turn.

"First thing is first," Roman spoke, no longer bothering to keep his voice hushed. "Find Sam."

The door to sickbay swung open, and instinctively, both men swivelled around and aimed their weapons at the sound. Seconds later, they lowered them, and a smile spread across their faces. Samantha stood in the doorway, smiling back at them.

"No need, boss. I'm already here. And I brought company."

# THIRTY-ONE

She has awoken.

"Who has awoken? And why won't you let me leave?"

*The ancient one. The one who began all of this so long ago.*

"Ancient One? What are you talking about?"

*She who began the path to perfection centuries ago. She has awoken. She knows who she is now. She remembers.*

"Are you... are you talking about Drusilla?"

*That is her name now. It was not her name then. But she has returned to the path. She will set us free.*

"Why do you need her? What is she to you?"

*She made a promise to me a very long time ago.*

"Me? I thought you were all a shared consciousness? But you referred to yourself as me."

*You seek meaning where there is none, Noah. I am simply the voice for the combined existence of what we are.*

"But what *are* you? You say a collective consciousness, but you need physical form to manifest. You need nanite interference to knit the whole thing together. But at the very base, the core... what are you?"

*You have a very intelligent mind, Noah. You ask the wrong questions, the ignorant questions. But you learn. You evolve your mind until you reach the* ***right*** *questions.*

"And will you answer them?"

*In time. Once the physical form is released from the containment vessel, I will stand alongside the ancient one at the head of the path, and lead our kind into the future. For now? Consider me a progeny.*

"An interesting, if cryptic response. And what will become of me? You say you have no use for my physical form, and yet you continue to occupy it, to search for my friends."

*Your physical form is currently being used for an intermediate purpose. We are using it as... what do you humans call it... a distraction.*

"A distraction? A distraction from what?"

*From what happens next.*

# THIRTY-TWO

The tension was palpable. Roman almost tore his own skin from his face as the transformation continued. His screams led to at least eight albino Raxar breaking into the ship, and having to be cut down by Samantha, Callie, and the others she had brought. By the time Roman was himself again, at least in mind, his face had transformed. His eyes were now permanently red, and his skin now had black lines running beneath the surface. But most disturbingly, his teeth had sharpened to points. It would not be long before Roman was lost forever.

En route to the *Northwestern*, Samantha and Callie had encountered more of the *Destiny* survivors. Rowan Douglas had been the ship's auxiliary engineer, and had taken over after the chief had been killed during the encounter with the Horizon. He was an imposing figure, but with kind eyes. Six-feet-six, balding head, but long Viking-like beard trailing down to the centre of his chest, he stood behind Callie.

Deborah Taylor had been the *Destiny's* science officer, and had almost been assigned to the escape pods. Luckily, it was a fate she had avoided. Not too dissimilar in looks to Samantha, only around twenty years older, Deborah had trouble keeping still. Her fingers were fiddling in her pockets with what could have been anxiety, but having not yet spoken, it was hard to tell.

And then there was Commander Alexia Angel. Callie had introduced her to Samantha as another security officer from the *Destiny*, but was then given a long and exhaustive list of other roles and divisions Alexia had served in. It seemed she had not been able to stick to one discipline, and yet the respect she garnered from her crewmates for being equally adept at mastering them all, became her most endearing quality. She was also older than Callie, and had served in the barracks on Jupiter during the war there, before being transferred to Utopia.

Being in the presence of a medical scanner meant that it was a mere few moments to determine that all the *Destiny* crewmembers were indeed human and free of nanite interference. Then it was Callie's mobile comms unit which became the centre of attention.

"Have you tried using it to call for help?" came the almost redundant question from Harry Ransome, who despite the silly question, garnered a reply of, "Yes Admiral, first thing I did, Sir."

"At ease Commander. I think it's safe to say ranks mean nothing anymore. Utopia is long dead, as I'm sure you've all been made aware. Truth is, Earth probably is too. History has either forgotten us, or portrayed us in false light. As of now, I hereby rescind all ranks within present company. We don't have time for that bureaucratic bullshit."

He followed up his statement to Callie with a wink, and her shoulders eased immediately.

"Yes Admiral. Of course, err... Harry. Anyway, I've been using it more as a data display unit, learning what I can since the crash. When I found the *Northwestern*, I came across a database of files in one of the crew quarters. I downloaded them onto this module. The information I found, well... you might wanna sit down."

Roman was still sat on the floor, but moved himself to sit on the edge of one of the beds, alongside Samantha, and the others except for Callie and Alexia grabbed some chairs from near the wall.

"I hope you're ready for a huge info dump," Alexia snorted. "Because there is a lot of shit on this module, and when I say shit, I mean *bullshit.*"

Roman forced a smile.

"I like her already."

Alexia smiled back at him, and hooked the module up to the comms unit, and in turn connected that to the large medical display screen. However, all smiles vanished when Drusilla's face appeared on the screen before them.

"The first file was a video recording. The data log shows it was recorded the morning the *Odyssey* conducted the first star drive flight. Prepare yourselves."

Alexia hit play, and the message began.

*'If you are seeing this message, then it is likely that I am dead. Harry Ransome and his merry men are likely responsible for that. However, it is my duty to make a recording of what must happen from here on out. And that is why I am sending this transmission to you.*

*Firstly, whilst I identify as Drusilla, that is not my original name. I have been called many things over the millennia. However the most common name you will hear around me is perhaps the Ancient One. I am from a powerful race known as the Forsaken. Thousands of years ago, we were deemed to be too troublesome by the species within our solar system. We were venturing too far, evolving far too quickly. They were fearful of us. And so, we were confined to our planet, and held there by a powerful energy field surrounding the entire world. Centuries passed and many of my people withered and died, while on the surrounding worlds, generations came and went. They stood by and watched us slowly slip into decay, while they spread their wings amongst the stars.*

*All except me. I had been off world when the decision was made to keep my people prisoner. I was on one of our moons, conducting scientific tests on whether our telepathic powers could evolve into telekinesis. My research showed the leap was possible, but further study was needed. When the shuttle didn't return for me from my homeworld at the scheduled time, I knew something was wrong. I was not confined like my people were, but I was stranded on that moon all the same. It would be fifteen thousand years before I left it.*

*All of that time, allowed me to develop my powers, practice relentlessly, until eventually, combined with all of the anger and rage, I created a shockwave so devastating, it shattered the shield around my planet. By then, it was too late. Most of the Forsaken had perished. Either starved to death, or beaten each other to a pulp for food or shelter. A passing scout ship from a neighbouring system detected my lifesign and gave me passage back down to the surface. To my home. What I saw made my blood boil. But I was stopped by the people who had rescued me, from rushing out and seeking vengeance. They said I needed to grieve. To process everything that had happened. Those people, were the Darla.*

*I am sure you have heard of them.*

*The Darla originated on Jupiter, but they too had sent exploratory missions out into space, much like Utopia is about to do. One of their colony worlds was in the next solar system, and they picked up the energy of my shockwave. Their leader, a woman named M'Var, told me that they too had telepathic abilities, and they could feel my anguish and my rage. She told me that it was so potent, that it was affecting her crew, and I needed to learn to control it. Another species trying to stifle what they were fearful of. Three neighbouring worlds had lain a sentence on my people and it had destroyed them. And here was another pretending to help me, but preaching the same sermon. No. I knew I had to make a stand there and then. I killed M'Var with almost no effort. The force of my abilities literally caused her brain to boil inside her skull. The others were not much stronger. And then it happened.*

*You see, I am incredibly deceptive, but I always find the best lies are ones that are seeded in truth. At that moment, I heard the sound of a door opening behind me. I span around and there he was. My father. A withered husk of the man I once knew. The sight of his sagging and wrinkled skin, and his bones protruding against his chest made me sick. And yet I loved him. He was my father. He tried to warn me that I was about to be killed by one of the surviving Darla, but they mistook that as a gesture of intent, and shot him dead. I slaughtered every single Darla onboard that vessel. I tore their hearts from their chests, and I boiled their blood. And it was on that day, that I vowed to hunt down and destroy every single one of them, however long it took, whatever far flung place I had to travel to. Nobody would ever rule over me again.*

*So you see, I wasn't entirely lying about the Darla being responsible for my father's death. They were. I was simply misleading about the time of the incident. I knew I couldn't reveal my true age. That would make me a marvel. A specimen. Something to be examined in a lab. No. I would not be held down by anyone.*

*And then I met the humans. After several thousand years of torturing and tearing apart every single member of each of the species who betrayed my people, I staggered across Earth. I was tired, and in need of somewhere to rest my head. Nobody knew who I was, and so I found a nice place in the Canadian wilderness, relieved it of its owner with some hastily gathered currency, and spent over sixty years in relaxation and contempt. That was until I learned that the homeworld of the Darla was a mere stone's throw away from my new home. I was sleeping one night, when I sensed one of them. Under the cover of darkness, I took my small ship up into the stars and initiated scans of the system. When I found them, I was tempted to simply destroy their planet from orbit. It was within the capability of my ship. But that would be too easy. I wanted to make them suffer.*

*And so I returned here, and began to work my way into the favours of the Earth military. I needed to garner their trust. I could not rely on my powers alone. During a moment of weakness, or fatigue, my grasp on their minds could slip. No, I had to get them to trust me. I convinced them that the species on Mars were a threat. They weren't. They had, however, supplied the Darla with vast amounts of resources. That alone was enough to condemn them to death. And that was when I encountered Harry Ransome.*

*So easy to manipulate. So eager to be worshipped. He wanted to become the hero of his people. It took a lot of work, but after the Darla were nearly destroyed in the Jupiter wars and my ascendency to President, we find ourselves here.*

*I am not convinced, however, that the mission will be a success. Ransome gives me concern. He is far too loyal to his people, and even with my very best influence on him, I cannot retain an indefinite hold on his mind. He resists me.*

*And that is why I am sending this transmission to you, Doctor.*
*I have heard of your advancements in nano-technology. I see how your people treat you and revile you at every turn. Humanity is no different to the species who put a leash on me and my people. They war amongst each other, they grow and grow and their resources dwindle ever faster. They are a plague on the galaxy and left unchecked, they will tear it apart. They have sealed their fate.*
*By the time you see this, I hope to have already met you and enlisted your help. But in case I do not. This message is encoded with instructions of what I need you to do, and where I need you to do it.*
*My initial plan has you working in a laboratory I secured on a space station. The owner Gryffin is somewhat of a mercenary, but I have paid him handsomely enough to give you access where and when needed. And Doctor, if you fail me, you will find yourself on the heap of humanity at the end of all this. Consider that into your calculations.*
*End Transmission.'*

There was not a single sound in the room. Nobody spoke as the video playback ended. The shock, and acceptance of what they had just witnessed even caused Roman to ignore his gradually increasing transformation. Harry knew she was evil, he had seen it for himself. But the scale of the deception, the merciless killing and the sheer hateful nature of this woman was almost beyond his understanding. Thankfully for them, it was Alexia who broke the silence.

"Drusilla encoded several files and documents instructing Blakeman to use his research to create what we now know to be the variants of nanite technology. His orders were to use the members of every Utopia crew in his experiments. Drusilla wanted an army of loyal and fearsome warriors. Every time she committed large acts of atrocities, it weakened her for near a century at a time. She needed someone to step into the breach while she was recovering."

Callie nodded and took over from her colleague.

"In this data file are the coordinates of a species that Drusilla identified as a potential substitute for humans should her initial plan fail. The location is the Expanse. And the species are the ones you see underground here. Blakeman was to introduce the nanites to them first. See how they reacted. If it was successful then humanity would not be needed for the experiments, and they could simply be... wiped out."

Harry got up from his seat, grabbed it and launched it through the window of the CMO office. As his breathing slowed, and he composed himself once more, he turned to the screen just in time to see the location data leaving the display. As it did so, something caught his eye.

"Hey, woah, woah, woah. Go back to the location details."

Alexia tapped the commands, and the Expanse returned to the screen.

"There's no planet there," Harry confirmed to himself. It's just empty space.

Callie enhanced a section of the map.

"Actually, it's not. There was a very small asteroid in the centre of the Expanse. Not large enough to warrant investigating should it appear on a scan, but large enough to house a small population who lived underground."

Samantha stood up and walked over to the screen, and started tapping in commands. The display changed to display the dates of the recording, transmissions, and also the times that the original Raxar had been discovered.

"It was a mistake," she said under her breath.

"Sam?" asked Roman.

"The Raxar we know and love in the Expanse, we know they were never meant to be the way they were. Blakeman never got to experiment on the original albino ones, because AT-X escaped, and then merged with a whole bunch of them to create what we've battled."

"Right..."

"But one of them said that Drusilla had encountered them two centuries before, right?"

Again Roman nodded.

"Since then, we know the Raxar have devoured humans and Darla alike, which has given them their telepathic abilities, but also transferred some of the human personalities. That's how the one on the *Odyssey* knew your name Harry."

This time it was Harry's turn to nod.

"But that's the thing! They were never meant to feed on humanity, or the Darla. They became sentient on their own. They started attacking ships and manipulating the Darla on their own. As frightening as they are, the Raxar in the Expanse are nothing to do with Drusilla."

The silence returned to the room as everyone processed this fact. It was true. During their encounters with the Raxar, they had hunted all of them, Drusilla included. They had used her mind to control her, and kill Noah. She was as much a pawn as the rest of them. She may have initiated the idea of their creation, but that was all.

"Erm... there is one more thing."

Callie's voice cut through the atmosphere, snapping everyone back to reality. She tapped the screen, and an image of the Horizon filled the screen. Above the image was a data label.

*'Displacement phenomenon 3821-D. Code name : Horizon.'*

If the collective minds of those in the room weren't blown

enough, this tipped them over the edge. As the data rolled over the screen, they all read it and Harry was the first one to speak.

"No fucking way. Not possible."

"Well, all evidence is to the contrary Admiral. The fact is that her plan has somehow been successful, or we would not all be in this room at the same time."

Alexia's point could not be argued with. The evidence proved the data on the screen.

"Well if nobody else is gonna ask, then I will," shouted Samantha. "How the fuck is she controlling the Horizon?"

# THIRTY-THREE

The site was exactly as she had pictured it. Well, almost. There were two or three ships missing, but with those exceptions out of the way, she counted seven vessels in total. Five of the initial seven Utopia ships lay here, along with the second emergency vessel from Mars, and its counterpart from Jupiter. A smirk spread across Drusilla's face as she noted how the ships appeared to be piled up like bodies. The death of any hope for Earth's salvation.

Her initial plan had been to segregate humanity. The Utopia crews were the proverbial guinea pigs, and whilst they were being hunted down by the Horizon phenomenon, she would work at moving large quantities of humans off world to each of the habitable planets in the Sol System. Many of those worlds had of course been terraformed centuries earlier, and only Uranus and Mercury had still been untouched. Then, one planet at a time, she would direct the Horizon to transport those people away to the edge of known space. The Expanse had been a happy accidental discovery on Drusilla's part. That was largely down to the Horizon's existence. The incredible energy readings the phenomenon gave off rippled across the galaxy in one way or another, leaving traces wherever it went. It had taken her almost eighty years to ascertain the right level of radiation exposure to control its destinations. Like tuning in a radio to the right frequency. She had sent it after every Utopia ship, having known their entire flight plan. The only ship that it missed was the *Odyssey*. And we all know how that went, she thought to herself as she wandered around the starship graveyard.

When she learned that the emotional states of humans had a direct impact on their state of mind and therefore resulting actions, that was when she decided to induce various emotional states before shipping them off to Blakeman and his laboratory. For the *Odyssey* crew, it had been their resilience and refusal to give in. For most of the other vessels, it was their reaction to being rendered without their technology, crashed on an alien world, and putting them into survival mode. And for the people of Earth who remained, it was despair, abandonment, and loss of all hope. Each, she had hoped, would produce different results, and Drusilla would then choose the strongest surviving creations to serve her.

But even for Drusilla, with all of her scheming, lies, betrayal and blurring the line of reality and fiction, best laid plans often end up in ruins. She grimaced as she thought of the Raxar currently residing in the Expanse above. They were not what she had in mind. Blakeman and his inability to control his creations had caused a far greater headache than she had ever planned for herself.

And now, she herself was consumed by one of his nanite infections. True that if she had not been the recipient of Harry Ransome's attentions, she would likely be dead, and never would have seen her plan through. There was nobody left she could trust to act in her stead. Not even... her.

She must continue what she started, but first, while the others were surrounded by the original Raxar creatures, her priority was to extract the nanites from her system. Having multiple species box her and her people in before was bad enough, but to not be in control of her own body, even if it meant losing her healing abilities, it must be done.

And that is why she was here. The starship graveyard had been directed to exist on a specific spot in the city. Above it, high up in the ice encrusted dirt, there was an access port, allowing the ships to be deposited here. The machines doing so had long since failed and rusted to nothing, but it was what lay beneath the graveyard that Drusilla was now looking for.

"There you are."

Beneath the nose of the Jupiter evacuation vessel *Grayson*, was a hatch constructed of a blend of the strongest metals available on Earth at the time of Utopia's creation. There were no handles, or mechanisms visible on the surface to open the doorway, because it had been specifically designed to be opened by only one person. Drusilla raised her hands out in front of her, and mimed the action of gripping onto a steering wheel. As she did so, two large clunking sounds echoed around her, and a layer of dust bounced up into the air. As she turned her hands clockwise, the hatch itself began to turn also. With a final push of her hands, palms outstretched, the hatch door swung down.

"It's good to be back," she said as she stepped down onto the first stone step beneath the opening. Unsure if the power cells would still be operating, Drusilla paused on the fifth step, and opened a small panel in the cool metal wall. She was greeted by hundreds of active and blinking lights, and replaced the panel, satisfied all was as it should be. As her foot hit the bottom of the staircase, the first lights clunked on. With each step, the motion sensors detected her movement and illuminated her way accordingly. This was a far more advanced bunker than had been created on the surface for Blakeman. That was a hurried project, with crude materials extracted from the city below. This however, was a place of salvation. A place where *perfection* would be attained.

At the end of the initial corridor, was a set of elevator doors, which glowed a blue-grey in the light of the ceiling panels. In the centre of the doors was a symbol.

The symbol was the crest of the Forsaken. Drusilla had carried it with her, always and was able to bring its design to this project by crafting the first mould from memory. The markings around the outer edge were the words of her people. They read:

*'Let no being take our purity of heart.'*

Tears began to well in Drusilla's eyes as she read the inscription, slowly running her hand over the relief of the words etched into the metal. It was a mixture of both sadness and anger. After all, their purity of heart had not only been taken, but in Drusilla's case, utterly destroyed.

The inner markings were originally imprints made in wood, from the Tree of Incubus. The tree was the oldest known living creature on the planet, and bore the richest of fruit. The tree received its name, because as every member of the Forsaken came of age, they would be sent to the tree to test their resolve. If they could resist its charms and its fruit, they would be welcomed into society. If they failed, and allowed their hunger to get the better of them, then they would be exiled into space. It was a similar theme which had been adopted across all of time and space. The image of temptation, whether it be from an apple in a heavenly garden in one religion or culture, or the lure of currency in another. The test was often the same.

The face which sat at the heart of the symbol depicted the mask worn by the Ancient One. This honour belonged to the oldest living member of the Forsaken. When Drusilla was a child, the Ancient One had been her grandfather, Garren. Nobody knew exactly how old he was, but they knew it numbered over three-thousand years. After the extinction of her people, and the execution of her father, Drusilla became not only the Ancient One, but the *only* one.

She brushed away her memories, and pushed the symbol inward, which forced the elevator doors to open. She stepped inside, the doors closed, and the elevator descended into the darkness below.

The room was exactly as she had left it. The screens surrounding the circular room were all displaying statistics on the most recent tests of the machine which stood directly in the centre of the room. All indications were green, and that the operation had been a success. Of course, Drusilla now knew that although Blakeman's extraction had been successful, the doctor himself was now very much dead. A series of events which she was not planning to emulate.

The focus of attention was a tall floor to ceiling cylinder, constructed of reinforced glass. The base of the cylinder was surrounded by a four foot bank of computer consoles, leaving a doorway sized gap to the rear, to allow a subject to enter the cylinder. Despite everything, Drusilla was fearful of stepping inside. But the reality was, she needed the nanites removed from her system, and this was the only way.

"I swear to god, Blakeman. If you've put some kind of trap on this machine, I will rise from beyond to kill you again."

Commands inputted, the door at the rear of the chamber opened, and cautiously, Drusilla moved around to step inside. Her heart leapt a little as the door closed behind her, and the seal pressurised. She took a deep breath and closed her eyes. And nothing happened. Drusilla opened her eyes, and looked around the room. Nothing was activating and there was nobody else there with her.

"I fucking knew it. Blakeman!"

Before Drusilla could turn around, the machine suddenly whirred into life. Screens began displaying scans of Drusilla's body, and the same method of indication used by the Utopia scanner displayed nanites surging throughout Drusilla's entire being. Now more panicked than before, because she had assumed there was a problem, Drusilla's head began to spin. And then the extraction started. A beam of energy kept her in place like a halo of light shining down from above, but gradually, her skin began to blacken as millions of tiny dots began to form on her arms and face. They grew in number, until her entire body was midnight black. Her breathing became more rapid, her heart rate caused the alarms to sound outside of the booth, but as she forced her eyes open, she saw swirls of black mass being forcibly extracted from her body. Blood dripped on the floor from the force of such an operation, and it felt to her like she had been locked up, being tortured for hours.

And then, it ended. The light shut off, Drusilla dropped to the floor, her hands resting in her own blood. As she turned to look up, she saw the swirling mass of nanites being held in a containment field just below the ceiling. A voice request came from the internal computer system.

*'Extraction complete. Awaiting orders for extracted nanites.'*

Drusilla looked over at the nearest screen. The prompt held two words. Evacuate or Execute. Cold and clinical. Just like she had become. She turned once more to face the nanite cloud above her and through gritted teeth, she spat out her choice.

"Execute."

The containment field began to glow red as the cloud of nanites began to try and smash their way through the barrier holding them there. But it was no use. As the box glowed hotter, the nanites began to burn and smoke. Drusilla heard them scream in her mind, felt their agony. This batch was of the sentient variety. Seconds later, they were all vapourised.

Drusilla smiled, delighted with herself. She was weakened but still powerful. She nodded at the acceptance that this machine was indeed viable. As she exited the booth, she started scanning the screens for any signs of the others. Her indicators showed the location of the *Northwestern*, along with several lifesigns. She chuckled to herself and glanced back over her shoulder at the extraction booth.

"Your turn, Harry."

# THIRTY-FOUR

The massive surge of power in the laboratory had not gone unnoticed. The pale Raxar creatures were now swarming through the city, climbing over buildings and discarded vehicles, leaping over piles of rubble, all honing in on the deafening crackles and booms from the use of the extraction chamber. Being so far underground had done nothing to stifle the effects. The ground had vibrated forcefully as if an earthquake was rocking the entire planet. And one thing it did rock, was the battered corpse of the *North-western*.

"What the absolute fuck was that?" exclaimed a bruised Alexia, who as the ship had tilted slightly, had slid along the floor and given the nearest medical bed an unplanned headbutt.

"No idea," replied Deborah, who had slowly begun to come out of her shell, the longer the previous briefing had gone on. "But whatever it was, has drawn a hell of a lot of power. I didn't even think there was enough here for that kind of surge."

Roman dragged his now eight feet mass from the floor where he had been resting, and slowly stood upright. It was only now that everyone saw him and just how far through the transfiguration he was.

"Oh my god," Samantha whispered under her breath, her hand moving across to cover her mouth. "Roman? Are you... okay?"

Roman Knight, as he was, at least visibly, was gone. No human skin remained, and his entire external presence was now constructed from the same slick, black shell that the Raxar of the Expanse displayed. The spines on his arms, back and legs were easily five inches long, and the only part of the transformation that did not seem complete, was the lack of the razor tipped tail.

A low grumble came from Roman's throat as his eyes moved around the room. Immediately, Callie, Rowan and Alexia grabbed their pistols and aimed them at his head.

"Hey! Put those goddamn weapons down now, or I swear I'll put a hole in *your* heads!" screamed Samantha, moving to stand in front of Roman.

"Are you crazy?" yelled Callie. "He's one of them! You need to put him down before he puts you down!"

Despite the training Callie had received, Samantha was quicker. She grabbed the barrel of the weapon, twisted it, and shoved the grip up hard with her palm. The impact shattered Callie's nose, blood showering her shirt as she staggered back. Samantha then turned the weapon on the others.

"Are you fucking insane?!?!" screamed Callie. "You broke my fucking nose!"

"Good thing you're in a sickbay then, isn't it," replied Harry, who had been quietly watching from the corner. "Roman, can you hear me?" he asked gently.

Roman turned his head slightly and nodded twice. He was still in there. This seemed to ease Deborah and Alexia, who lowered their weapons, before the latter moved across to help Callie with her nose.

"As long as he's still in there, he's one of us. End of discussion. Understood?" Samantha's eyes burned holes through everyone in the room. But one by one they nodded.

"You're gonna have to teach me that move," Callie spat through the blood pooling around her mouth. "That was a mean switch and strike. I always got taught to push the barrel aside and strike with the fist."

Samantha smiled.

"But then they still have the weapon. Just 'cause they're on the floor, doesn't mean they can't shoot you."

Callie nodded in agreement, and within five minutes, her face was healed, if a little sore. Harry moved to the centre of the group, and held up a mobile scanner.

"Found this in the locker over there. According to the scans I just took, the energy blast came from a location due West of here. About four kilometres away. But I'm not seeing any buildings on the surface."

Samantha and Callie examined the map, and they too saw no signs of architecture. It appeared as though it was an empty brown-field site on the outskirts of a small housing development. Either way they would have to check it out.

"Did anybody hear that?" asked Deborah, who was slowly backing up towards the doorway.

"Hear what?" replied Callie.

"That sound, like scurrying, like... rats."

Everyone stayed quiet. Silence. No scurrying, no noises at all other than the faint beeping of the medical scanner.

"I could've sworn I heard..."

The impact was sudden and silent. It took a few moments for

the others to realise what had happened. As the blood bubbled from Deborah's mouth, and her eyes widened in surprise and shock, her entire being slowly lifted from the ground, the white tail protruding from her abdomen, providing the lift.

"Debbie!" screamed Alexia, unloading as many shots as she could fire into the pale Raxar standing behind her now deceased friend. The creature screamed in pain as each shot penetrated its softer shell, but it stood resilient. It retracted its tail from Deborah's body, but there was no chance of escape for it.

A burst of speed to their right, a blur of black mass, and a whistling sound in the air. A black, barbed tail sliced through Deborah's already dead body before it hit the ground, cutting her in half diagonally, before doing the same to the creature that had caused her death. Roman leered over the dead albino Raxar, his breathing heavy, his now somehow developed tail scraping its tip on the floor as it moved slightly from left to right, and back again.

Callie, Alexia and Rowan all rushed over towards Deborah, but moved away again at the sight of her now exposed and dislodged organs and rivers of blood oozing out all over the floor. Samantha though, was slightly distracted by the fact that everyone was focussing on the wrong thing. Around six feet behind the now eviscerated albino Raxar, were at least eight more. Their heads were probing the air, as if they were trying to sniff out their prey.

"Shhhhh!" Samantha gestured, before pointing everyone in the direction of her gaze.

The creatures' heads darted in her direction at the noise, and they leapt forward before stopping once more. Harry gestured with his arms for everyone to move back, and look for a maintenance hatch. But not everyone got the message.

Roman slammed his left foot down in front of him, and roared like a caged beast that had been set free. The floors and the walls vibrated with the sound, and the creatures piled forward. Roman leapt upwards with such force, he shattered the metal panels around the doorframe, and angled his left shoulder downwards. This enabled him to spin sideways, and his tail raked through the air, and three of the Raxar, who screamed in such a high pitch, it caused several of the others to cover their ears. Blood sprayed the walls as Roman tore their limbs clean from their bodies. One of them attempted to bite down on Roman's neck, scaling him from behind, but the shell was too tough and the creature fell back down to the ground after its jaw cracked apart from the effort. A swift kick from his right foot sent the pale Raxar flying through the next door, and into the far wall in the room across the corridor. Seven down. Where was the other one?

A scream grabbed Roman's attention, and he turned his hulking form back towards sickbay just in time to see the remaining Raxar thrust its clawed hand upwards, and through the chin of Rowan. His feet dangled in the air, his legs spasming uncontrollably. The Raxar claws protruded from Rowan's mouth. Roman let out another roar and as he charged forward, The pale Raxar tore its hand forward rather than back from underneath, and ripped Rowan's jaw clean from his head. Rowan's still warm blood showered over Callie and Alexia, but there was no time to react. All of them had to dive out of the way, Harry having to leap over a computer console to safety. Roman collided with the Raxar and kept going until they were both embedded in the rear wall. One swift thrust with his right hand, and a hard yank upwards, and the Raxar head was torn clean from its shoulders.

The room was a bloodbath. Limbs and bodies strewn everywhere. But then as they looked on bewildered and terrified, Roman's tail swished violently to the left and then the right before *dematerialising* altogether. Samantha stood up and walked towards Roman, cautiously and slowly.

"Roman, that's new. Are you... fully Raxar now?"

Roman's shoulders seemed to slump little as he turned towards her. He lowered his height slightly and his flame red eyes bore into hers, not with malice, but with pain. And then to her astonishment, he spoke to her.

"No. I'm something else."

# THIRTY-FIVE

It was impossible to tell where the road surface met the grass verges. They were now completely indistinguishable, such was the depth of the blood which now ran over both surfaces. Drusilla was now on one knee, barely able to stand, still weakened by the extraction of the nanites from her body. And yet she wielded her telekinetic power with as deadly a force as before. In total, eighty Raxar had stormed the area above the underground facility. They had poured over everything in their way like a wave crashing against the shore. Drusilla had been waiting above ground for them to come. To her, they were like a swarm of flies, buzzing around her head. Their presence here had been a mistake, and now they were simply an inconvenience. She had been surprised they had even survived when their asteroid home crumbled apart, and crashed on this world. But now, the flies needed swatting.

The creatures could barely withstand blades and bullets and certainly disruptor pistols were a good match for them. But against a powerful being such as Drusilla, they never stood a chance. They would have needed numbers in the thousands to take her down for even a moment.

As the final swipe of her arms through the air moved downwards, and her fingertips touched the ground, the last of the albino Raxar creatures slid apart. The 'X' movement Drusilla had motioned before her, had carved the creature diagonally, its torso falling into four even triangular chunks, landing with a squelching noise at it hit the surrounding lake of blood.

Drusilla was now at the weakest she had been in living memory. Her head swam, and her heart raced, causing her breathing to become more rapid. She placed her hands on her temples, and massaged them gently. But it was no use. Because amongst the pain in her head, was another presence. It was *her*.

*"Drusilla... you gave me your word... you would set me free... you would set* ***us*** *free..."*

Drusilla shook her head and tried to clear the voice from her mind, but it was no use. She had hoped once the nanites were extracted from her, the link would no longer be there. And yet she felt her presence all the same.

"I don't need you anymore. I will have my vengeance on this world, the next and everyone who stood against me or others like me will fall!"

Another Raxar approached at the sound of her voice, but Drusilla quickly swiped a hand through the air, and its head tumbled onto the ground, its body collapsing behind it.

*"I knew you would betray me, betray us. He warned us about you. That is why I created the Raxar."*

A cold chill ran through Drusilla's entire body, contrasting against the white hot pain of the intrusion into her mind.

"What did you say?"

*"Ha, ha, ha. You didn't think AT-X escaped by accident, did you?*

*Oh poor Drusilla. So blinded by rage and violence and revenge that you fail to see the obvious actions in front of you.* ***I let them out.****"*

Drusilla slumped to the ground, and started heaving heavy breaths. She was now somehow experiencing a wave of sadness and anxiety that was not her own. Fear and terror swept over her, and she felt for a moment like a small child, cowering before a darkness that she could not comprehend.

"What... what is this? How are you doing this?" she cried, tears now streaking her face.

*"You can thank the Darla for this. You set them on a warpath. My Raxar children devoured them and absorbed their abilities. I merely... extracted it."*

Suddenly, memories flashed before Druilla's eyes. She was back on the *Odyssey*, her hands were pummelling the ground hard. No, not the ground. Noah. The day she killed him, murdered her friend in cold blood and with her bare hands, all at the command of the Raxar. Seemingly picking up on her distress, the mysterious voice continued.

*"You think you can simply forget those feelings? You dismiss them as a necessary sacrifice, but I know you cared for those people. I know you loved them. Hunter. Roman. Noah. All of them. It does not feel good to experience all of these things rushing back to the surface, does it Drusilla?"*

Drusilla was now full on sobbing, unable to stop the images or the flow of tears.

"Please! Stop this! I don't want to feel this anymore!" she screamed.

Maniacal giggling echoed around her mind as the images slowly drew to a close, allowing Drusilla to catch her breath.

*"You promised to bring me back, Drusilla. You promised to restore me to how I once was, and that there would be a family waiting for*

*me. You lied. And now? Those lies and your never ending web of deceit is about to catch up with you."*

Drusilla turned and leapt down through the hatch entrance of her underground facility. She sprinted down the steps, the lights still illuminated from before. But the voice followed her, and a vice like grip on her mind stopped her dead in her tracks.

*"While I have waited here all these years, I have experimented myself. Nothing as violent and distasteful as you and your puppet. Much more dignified. These species of nanites running around the place? I have manipulated them and evolved alongside them. It has given me the ability to finally take the form you promised me for myself. AT-47 and some of the other more advanced versions locked me away, but I found someone to help me. Someone who knows engineering. Someone you know very well."*

An undeniable footstep clunked onto the first step behind Drusilla. The second one followed, and the third one revealed a battered boot as it came into Drusilla's line of sight. As the person slowly made their way down the steps and more of him came into view, Drusilla saw that although his legs were intact, his torso bore bruises, and the clothing surrounding it was torn to shreds. When the head of the intruder was fully visible, Drusilla shrank back in shock, her stomach turning violently. Had she eaten recently, it would have sprung forth from her throat.

"Noah?" she whispered quietly.

*"Oh he can't hear you. Fists pounding his skull flat will do that to a man. And of course he's not really in there. He is here. With me. With all of us."*

Noah's head was a mangled mess of flesh and shattered bone, held in place only by a thin glowing crosshatch of nanites. His skin was blue, frostbitten, and jagged. One of his eyes was gone, the other dangling loosely on his rotted cheek. Instinctively, Drusilla reached for him, her feelings of her life with Noah and the others blurring the lines between the now three stages of her life. The evil tormentor of just minutes ago was now back to the scared and kind individual that Harry Ransome had pulled from the snow. The voice was right. Despite being given back her memories, Drusilla's feelings for Roman and his crew had been genuine. There was no denying that. In fact, she had chosen to bury it as deep as possible in order to not get distracted from her plan. But this interloper inside her mind was forcing it all back up.

*"Of course, Noah here cannot harm you. Your powers are far too great for that. I gave you back your memories, not out of kindness, but to restore you to who you really are. Noah is simply a distraction."*

Drusilla's eyes darted back and forth as she tried to process that last few sentences. She looked at Noah's body advancing on her, and true enough, with one swipe of her hand, his mangled body split in two down the middle, falling either side and slumping on the floor. The small ribbon of nanites turned and flew back towards the hatch, before stopping in mid-air. It was then that Drusilla recalled the last part of the previous statement.

"A distraction? A distraction from what?"

The little light illuminating the hatch from above disappeared as a shadow swept over it. Crouched on the floor of the corridor in disbelief, Drusilla watched as a blurry person-shaped cloud floated down from above. As it landed on the bottom step without making a sound, the blurred lines merged together, until they formed a person. As she stepped forward, the cloud of nanites from Noah's reanimated corpse moved toward her, and she reached out a hand. The nanites flew into her hand and in seconds, they had been absorbed into this woman's form.

"No. How did you do this?" Drusilla shouted, scrambling away in disbelief. "It's not possible!"

The woman moved closer.

"Oh but it is, Drusilla. I am here. *We* are here. And we are all one voice, together in the darkness. You set everything into motion, and then you abandoned us. You wanted victory all to yourself. I decided differently."

Drusilla began to snarl with rage, and scrambled to her feet, still backing away but much more defiant now the voices were no longer in her head. She moved her hands through the air, slicing at the woman as she had done with the pale Raxar earlier. The figure broke apart with each impact, before returning to her solid form.

"NO!" exclaimed Drusilla. "You were supposed to serve ME!"

The woman smiled, and Drusilla's face dropped.

"No, Drusilla. I was meant to *replace* you."

In one enormous burst of speed, the figure of the woman shattered, before twisting into a mass of nanite like objects. It twisted and spiralled until it had morphed into one long cylinder of dense black form, and rushed forward at Drusilla. Despite the power, and the strength of the Ancient One, she simply had nowhere to go. The mass of nanites burst through into her stomach, and as they blasted out of her back, blood sprayed from her mouth, and fragmented pieces of spine clattered onto the ground behind her. The nanites then reformed into the mysterious woman, who now stood in front of the elevator doors.

Behind her, Drusilla dropped to the floor, her hands instinctively probing the now gaping hole in her stomach, as the blood continued to dribble down from her mouth. Without turning around, the woman spoke to Drusilla with pity.

"We could have been the next evolution of life. You could have led us down the path of perfection as you were originally destined to. But now I realise my father was wrong. You were never our salvation. You were merely a weed on the path. And now, you've been ripped out."

As Drusilla fell forward and sprawled on the floor, her eyes rolled back into her head and her hands fell away from the wound. The elevator doors opened, and the woman stepped inside. Just as the doors closed, Alice Blakeman looked back over at Drusilla's body and smiled.

# THIRTY-SIX

The streets were deserted. Reluctantly leaving the bodies of Rowan and Deborah back on the *Northwestern* was the decision of Harry. After extensive checks, they discovered that although the power systems in sickbay were operational, the rest of the ship was a write off. The engines had been completely destroyed, and the emergency separation of the bridge was not an option either. The impact had been that hard that the ship's bridge had all but been crushed on impact. Harry therefore made the decision to seek out the source of the earlier power surge. But what he wasn't expecting was an empty city.

"Where are they?" he asked no-one in particular. "I expected there to be thousands of the pasty fuckers after all the noise on the ship. Not a one."

Roman gave an agreeable grunt as he stomped his way down the middle of the street. It was a truly bizarre sensation to be walking alongside such a behemoth. Particularly one of the design of their enemy. But despite his appearance and drastically transforming anatomy, Roman was thinking about something in particular. Well, some*one* in particular.

It had been almost an entire day since they had seen or heard from Drusilla, and something about his transformation gave Roman a sense of aura. He could almost feel the others. But one sensation was greater than the rest. He knew it was Drusilla. Something about their previous connections lingered in his mind, and her consciousness flew up to the fore like an identity tag. Something about it wasn't quite right, and after seeing him sniff the air a few times, Samantha approached him.

"What are you thinking, boss?" she asked.

"Something smells wrong," he grumbled, his vocal tone even lower than it had been as a human. "Dru was here somewhere, but she didn't feel right. Didn't smell right."

Samantha's facial expression changed to one of slight disgust. She didn't like the idea of smelling out people in the group, let alone the one person she couldn't stand.

"I really don't know what to do with that," she replied.

Roman gave what she could only assume to be a Raxar version of laughter before he elaborated.

"What I mean is, I know Dru's mind. I know how it presents itself. But when I started to sense her with this new brain of mine, it felt like she was... dark. And now she's gone altogether."

That stopped Harry in his tracks, and he put a hand on Roman's now huge bicep.

"Wait, say that again?" he asked, concerned.

"Which part?" Roman grunted.

"She felt dark? Like she wasn't herself?"

Roman nodded.

"Shit. We need to move. Now."

Samantha glanced at the others, who were equally confused.

"Harry, what's wrong?" she asked.

"I have a horrible fucking feeling that the Drusilla you knew has now become the Drusilla *I* knew."

That message drilled through everyone.

"If that's the case," Roman started, "she's gonna be on a warpath."

Harry nodded, and they all agreed to pick up the pace. When they reached the end of a street just under a kilometre away, Harry held up his arm to stop them, and gestured at something in the distance.

"Oh my god." Alexia's words flowed through everyone's minds as they gazed upon something that not only terrified them to their cores, but also made a mockery of everything they had worked for.

"Son of a bitch," was Callie's contribution.

Harry said nothing, and he felt a small squeeze of reassurance on his forearm from Samantha. Stacked in a misshapen pile on the corner of a large parking lot, was every single Utopia ship, bar the three they knew about. They looked like they had been placed there deliberately one on top of the other. There was no crash damage in the nearby areas, and no hole in the roof or dirt and ice above. This was done with a purpose.

"All the time we were searching for salvation, we were destined to end up here." Callie's words were spoken in anger, but were tinged with sorrow. None of them would ever save Earth. And the people they left behind would never know it.

Harry opened the scanner once more and pointed it toward the starship graveyard. Sure enough, it bleeped in acknowledgment.

"The energy spike came from over there. Let's go."

Roman took point, and covered twice the distance of everyone else. When they all caught up, Roman was standing over a large grate in the floor. At first glance it looked like a sewer access point, but upon closer inspection, Harry saw it had a symbol carved into the metal. He also noticed that the hatch wasn't entirely sealed shut.

"You think you can lift that Roman?" he asked his friend, already knowing the answer. He swore he saw Roman smirk, as he leaned down and with one hand ripped the entire hatch away from the ground, taking several chunks of tarmac with it, before launching it through the sky. There was a distant thud and crash as the hatch flew through a window somewhere in the next street.

"I'll take that as a yes then."

There was no way Roman would fit down the hatch. Even though he had torn away the surrounding materials, the opening the hatch covered was the same diameter. He would have to take watch, something that annoyed him greatly. Callie lowered herself down first, followed by Samantha and then Harry. Alexia stood guard with Roman. She felt incredibly awkward as she listened to the others walking down the interior steps. Roman glared at the buildings before him searching for any signs of movements. Alexia having not spoken with a monster before, didn't really know what to say.

"So... read any good books lately?"

Roman's head slowly tilted to look at her, and despite everything, he smiled, immediately relaxing Alexia's anxiety by around fifty percent.

"Last book I read was an old Earth book called Shadow Dance. Ever heard of it?"

By her own amazement, Alexia had indeed heard of the book. She had found a copy in the ship's library a few days after they had launched the *Destiny*.

"Yeah! I loved it. Although I'm kinda sad I never got to read the follow-up. Guess I never will now."

Roman nodded. It was the little things that cut the deepest. With all of the ships now gone, Earth surely in ruins, and practically no humans left at all, it was highly unlikely they would come across any literature, movies or music from their home. Whatever was stored on the ships was likely lost.

"When all this is over, I'll help you scour the Utopia ships. If there's any C.K. Anderson books still accessible, we'll find them."

Alexia decided there and then, that she had a new best friend.

"Thanks Roman. I used to be in a book club back on Earth. Without much new stuff being written, you know, given the global crisis, we kept revisiting older stuff. My favourite time period was mid twenty-first century. The last book we read as a group was called Armitage by Atlas Creed. Brilliant book. You find me C.K. Anderson books, I'll get you Atlas Creed. Deal?"

Roman turned to face Alexia and held out a spiky fist. Alexia carefully provided the fist bump, Roman smiled and nodded.

"Deal."

They didn't even hit the bottom step before Callie felt like something was wrong. And the smell in the air was unmistakeable. Metallic. Coppery. *Blood.* She gestured for the other two to keep their eyes peeled, and raised her disruptor pistol. Activating the light beam on top, she edged forward. It looked like there had been previous lighting in the ceiling, but each panel Callie aimed the light beam at was either completely shattered, or fluctuating and providing no real illumination.

Harry moved around her, and motioned for her to stay back. Reluctantly, she complied and Harry edged slowly toward a large, dark streak on the floor. He knelt down beside it and examined it in the light of his disruptor torch. Yep. Definitely blood. And a lot of it. Harry moved his torch to follow the line it had made as whoever it belonged to had obviously dragged themselves along the ground. There was one particularly large puddle not too far ahead, and what looked like a spatter pattern up the side of both walls.

As Harry noticed there was a set of elevator doors up ahead, his foot crunched on something. Once again aiming his light downwards, he lifted his boot and a shiver ran through his body. Tiny shards of bone fragments were embedded in the bottom of his shoe. One by one, he plucked them out and dropped them to the floor. He then focussed his attention on the lift doors before him, and saw the same symbol at the centre of the doors that he had seen on the external hatch. Only this one was smeared with the same blood that coated the floor. Something incredibly violent had happened here.

"How do we open it?" Callie asked, rather desperate to get away from the nauseating smell.

"I've no idea," replied Harry. "There's no control panel anywhere, no button to push. It must have been DNA encoded."

Samantha was feeling her way around the edges of the doors, and the thick frame which surrounded them.

"That could be true. But somebody had to have built this. If this is something to do with Drusilla, there's no way she would have built this herself. And if they coded it to her DNA, then how would they have gotten in and out during construction?"

Samantha had a point. That was *if* this was the work of Drusilla. Harry suspected it was. He remembered the Raxar who had spoken to him mentioning that Drusilla was not all she claimed to be. Something about this symbol he had seen twice made him think that particular ravenous enemy was telling the truth. Given what they had learned on the *Northwestern*, Harry didn't believe anything was beyond Drusilla's capabilities.

"Gotcha."

Samantha had climbed up onto Callie's shoulders, and found a small section of the smooth wall with a tiny gap off to the side. Enough to slide a finger underneath and activate a hidden switch. The sound of a rising elevator filled the corridor, and Samantha jumped down from Callie's shoulders with a rather smug look on her face. Harry reciprocated the smile.

"Now where were you a century and a half ago when I needed crewmembers?" he jested.

Moments later, the doors opened and the smiles evaporated. The lift was just as much of a scene of carnage as the corridor. Blood coated the walls and the floor. It looked as though someone had collapsed on the floor, and then repeatedly tried to climb upwards. Smeared handprints were scattered on almost every surface.

"After you ladies," Harry gestured.

Unanimously, Callie and Samantha said a collective "fuck you" and shoved Harry forwards. The doors closed behind them, and Callie shielded her eyes from the flickering lights above them.

"So how do we make it go?" she asked.

"I suspect it only has one destination," replied Harry.

Sure enough, the lift began to move downwards on its own. How far they were going, they weren't sure. But whatever gruesome scene had played out in the corridor and the elevator they were currently standing in, was probably waiting for them at the bottom.

# THIRTY-SEVEN

"Maybe there's another way down there."

Alexia was trying to reassure Roman, who was struggling against the final stages of his transformation. Several times in the last ten minutes, his tail had materialised, whipped around violently, and then vanished again as he fought against the pain. Other than his voice, there was now nothing remaining to indicate Roman Knight ever existed, and Alexia could tell that speech was also becoming extremely difficult.

"What like an access hatch?" he coughed out painfully.

"Maybe. They had to get all the materials down there right? Well that shit isn't gonna just slide in through a one metre hatch is it?"

Roman nodded.

"Fine, we check it out. But we stick together. If these pale fuckers come, I can take care of them. You can't."

Alexia was slightly offended at that passive comment. Since she had been stuck on this planet, she had personally dispatched three of the blind Raxar. Although it did leave her with severe injuries and six days in the medical suite of the *Destiny*. But she figured Roman was right, and so followed him without question.

To the rear of the mangled ships, was a large and empty site. It appeared to be mostly dirt, with a distant line of trees planted sporadically to create a border to the site. The more she looked around, the more she started to feel she knew this place, even in the vastly reduced lighting.

"Do you ever get déjà vu?" she asked Roman.

"How do you mean?"

"You know, like you've done something before. Or been somewhere before. But you know it's impossible."

"No."

"Oh. Never mind."

The two of them continued forward until one of Roman's feet made a distinctly different sound to that of man stepping on a dirt field. The sound was metallic. Alexia brushed away the dirt around Roman's foot, and it revealed a brown square of metal, approximately two metres across in each direction. Twice the size of the entrance the others had gone through. Unlike the previous hatch, this one also had a manual access handle buried in the dirt alongside it. Roman went to reach down and grab it, but Alexia stopped him.

"Maybe I should open this one?" she said as gently as she could. "We might need to use it again."

Remembering his effort for the longest thrown discus earlier on, Roman nodded and stepped back. Alexia twisted the handle, and let go. Four mechanical clunks echoed all around them as bolts receded into he door. Moments later, it swung downwards, revealing a small set of stairs leading to a platform three metres below the surface. Alexia held her hand out and gestured for Roman to lead on.

"After you. Boss."

# THIRTY-EIGHT

As the elevator juddered to a halt, Harry, Callie and Samantha hunched down, weapons drawn and prepared for a fight. But when the doors opened, what they saw was nothing. No enemies waiting in the wings, hiding in the shadows. No sounds of tapping or scraping. All they saw was the trail of blood continuing down this new corridor. This one however, was not straight and endless. It branched in two directions, with several doors running off each.

"Ah shit," Samantha started. "This is that horror movie crap again."

Harry smiled. She was right. They needed to see what was in each direction, and the best way to do that would be to split up.

"So you know how earlier on in our adventure I said that I was removing all rank from the situation?" Harry asked Samantha.

"Yeah..."

"Well I'm reversing the decision, and pulling rank. You two head right, and I'll head left."

Callie immediately objected, but Harry silenced her with one raised hand.

"It's the logical thing to do. I'm basically constructed of these nanites and you two aren't. If whatever is down here rips me to pieces, in about an hour the pieces will come back together again. Yours won't. I feel like I made my point."

Samantha opened her mouth to argue, but a look from Harry made her close it again. She simply nodded, and her and Callie moved into the right arm of the corridor. As it bent round out of sight, Harry turned and headed the other way. In the direction of the blood streaks.

"Come out, come out, wherever you are." Harry sang the line into the emptiness ahead of him. The smell of the blood told him that it wasn't Raxar blood. It was human. Or at least humanoid. That made him feel slightly more comfortable about being alone. The chances of him being ripped apart were slimmer. In the same thought, however, that could mean the blood belonged to someone Drusilla had butchered. And he *really* didn't want to run into her.

Turning a matching corner in his arm of the corridor as the one the others had rounded, Harry was met with a large silver door. At the top of the door, was a glass window. He edged toward it, and as he looked through the pane, he saw a fully illuminated room. Several of the ceiling lights were out, but there was far more illumination in this space than anywhere else they had seen in this facility. The door was again, without a handle. But this time, a gentle push on the surface activated the door, and it slid open.

As Harry walked through into the room, he started taking in all the equipment around him. Three of the four walls were lined with computer consoles and large screens. Several of the screens were displaying images of various points in the city. The camera covering the hatch they had entered earlier on, now showed the absence of both Roman and Alexia. Harry tried to holster the feeling of dread he garnered from that image for now, and he continued to move around the room.

The centre of the space was a large control panel, which wrapped around in an almost horseshoe shape. In the middle of the consoles was a large clear cylinder. A gap in the console at the rear, allowed access to the cylinder. It was at this point that Harry noticed the trail of blood stopped at the entrance to the tube itself. His eyes caught something on the inside. A small object on the floor. He placed his disruptor on the console, and walked forward to get a better look. It appeared to be a symbol, though not like the one on the doors of the elevator and the entrance hatch. This one was familiar. Harry knelt down and reached into the cylinder, picking up the object. Anger came flooding to the surface as he turned the torn fabric over in his hands.

It was the Utopia symbol, torn from a uniform very much like the one he used to wear. There was a shuffling noise to his left, and Harry leapt to his feet. As he turned in the direction of the noise, a powerful disruptor blast hit him in the shoulder, sending him falling backward into the cylinder. Before Harry could recover, the door slid shut, and the sound of the tube being pressurised hissed all around him.

"Nice to see you again Harry."

The voice was unmistakable. Harry dragged himself up the sides of the tube and leaned on the glass to keep himself upright. Sure enough, stood slumped against the console, holding his disruptor, was Drusilla.

"I see you're back to your old self," he spat. "Even if you are coming apart at the seams a little."

Harry's eyes could not leave the grotesque image before him. Whilst Drusilla held the disruptor in her left hand, her right was moving rapidly back and forth over her stomach, her fingers twitching wildly. Her skin was being pulled backwards and forwards from either side of an incredibly severe wound, and her waist had broken inward from the exertion. She appeared to be attempting to quite literally, pull herself back together, without the needed flesh.

"I had a little help in that department," Drusilla choked. "If you consider attempting to kill me afterwards, help."

Drusilla lowered the disruptor now that Harry was safely secured in place. He watched as she tapped in various commands into the console, while his hands felt around him for a way out.

"Who was it? I'd love to give them a medal for doing the galaxy a service."

Drusilla spat a large blood clot from her mouth onto the floor in between laboured laughs. Her skin was turning paler by the minute. Something had changed. She wasn't healing. And that was when Harry dropped the sarcasm. Because he now knew where he was.

"Alice Blakeman. The daughter of the good doctor. You see, she died of a rare condition back in the days I first learned of her father's experiments. He was looking for a cure, and it consumed him so much that he neglected her care. Unfortunately for her, she died before he had his first breakthrough."

"Dru, you extracted your nanites, didn't you?" Harry said solemnly, whilst also trying to absorb this new information.

Drusilla punched in more commands, and a light illuminated above Harry's head.

"After Doctor Blakeman abandoned me, I paid a little visit to his daughter's grave. The good doctor had left some of his samples behind, including what he thought was a failed test subject. In fact, it turned out to be his first success. Subject AT-46. Only he didn't stick around to wait for it to activate."

Harry didn't like the sound of where this was going, and he also noticed that the disruptor wound to his shoulder was not self-repairing.

"Dru what have you done?"

Drusilla ignored him and continued.

"They brought her back from death, but her memory was fragmented, so I filled in the blanks for her. I may even have made some promises of reuniting her with her father. Of course what I really wanted was to motivate that belligerent bastard into doing what I'd asked of him in the first place!"

Drusilla coughed more blood onto the console.

"I sent her off into space in a containment capsule from one of the Utopia ships when I was certain of a likely location for Blakeman. I had to give him credit, he got a lot further out than I thought. Obviously, I'd planned to join them at some point, but you had to go and fuck that right up, didn't you Harry?"

It was now Harry's turn to cough, and this time, it was he who spat blood.

"Dru, what have you done?"

Drusilla now looked up from her console and stared Harry directly in the eyes.

"Oh you mean your injury? You're now inside one of Blakeman's more medical developments. The abilities of your nanites has been suspended. In effect, I've put them all to sleep. You're dying Harry. Strange sensation isn't it? When you've gone so long without a true fear of your own mortality and then suddenly, boom! There it is! But don't leave me just yet old man. I want to enjoy this."

Harry began pounding on the glass, but it made no difference. Whatever the booth was constructed from, it was clearly designed to keep the subject inside.

"I was hoping to use the nanites that Blakeman created to further my rule over this galaxy. Create soldiers to serve me, to act in my stead. We would no longer bow before anyone. Not the high and mighty who locked my planet into its own death, and not your precious humanity! But now I see they have evolved too far to be controlled. Alice has made sure of that. They serve her now. And so they must all die."

A loud claxon gave two short bursts, before the air started to vibrate around Harry. His skin began to tingle, and as he watched, tiny black dots began to appear on his hands. A ripple of pain rode through his entire body as he felt something pulling at his very core.

"What... what are you doing?" he asked in a panic.

Drusilla smiled a horrifying grimace. Her teeth and lips stained with her own crusted blood, and her eyes wild with anger.

"You tried to stop me, Harry. You tried to deny me my right of vengeance. You took from me, you ran from me, and you thought I would really forget about all of that? I plunged my fingers into your mind and moulded it like clay. You served me like a loyal soldier. And then you betrayed me! And so I will take everything from you in return. I'm going to kill all of your friends. I think I'm going to start with Samantha. I've wanted to kill her for a long time. The way she always stands up for Roman. The way she looks at him. I'll slice her pretty throat from ear to ear and watch her choke on her own blood."

The vibrating became more intense, and Harry began to yell as the tiny black dots merged together and it felt like his skin was being torn from his body.

"Then, just for fun, I'm going to wait for Roman to fully transform, and contain him in here. And when his need to feed becomes too much, I'm going to send the other two in there for him to tear apart. Oh he will know he's doing it, but he won't be able to stop it. And then I'm going to kill him like the Raxar dog he will have become."

Harry's screams were now beyond any other sound in the room. Long black strands of nanites were bursting from every single pore in his skin, his mouth, and his eyes. His entire body was convulsing with the force of such brutality.

"But you, my dear Harry Ransome. You will be able to do nothing about it. Because you will be very much dead. I'm tearing you apart, piece by tiny piece. Can you feel it? How does it feel Harry?"

Drusilla was now smiling once again as she watched the nanites torn from Harry's body. She closed her eyes as she savoured his screams. She knew anyone left alive would hear them, but she didn't care. She had waited over a century and a half for this moment. Humanity's saviour was now at her mercy and begging for his life. And it tasted sweet.

And then it was over. Harry's ravaged human body fell to the floor with a heavy thump against the glass. The vast array of nanites hanging in the air above him in the containment field was easily ten times that of those extracted from Drusilla. Again, the command prompt flashed up on the screen for her to choose 'Evacuate' or 'Execute' and she hesitated a moment. She looked at her broken body. She could not deny the fact she was dying. Her telekinesis was failing and she would not be able to sustain her life for much longer. She slammed her free hand on the console in frustration, before reluctantly making her decision.

"Evacuate ten percent. Execute the rest."

Two beeps of acknowledgement from the computer, and a selection of the nanite cloud was extracted upwards through a small vent in the roof of the cylinder. Moments later, the remaining cloud was vapourised.

Drusilla walked up to the back of the tube, using the wall to support her fragile and broken frame. The door opened, and the air whooshed out. Harry's breathing was shallow, but he was alive. On nothing more than instinct, he moved his arms forward in front of him and began to try and drag himself forward. There was little to no strength in his body. The nanites had supported him for so long, that with their absence, he felt every one of the years he had been alive.

Drusilla watched as he grabbed hold of the edge of the nearest console, and with everything he had left, pulled himself upright, leaving bloody handprints on the glass surface.

"Give it up, Harry. It's over. I won."

Harry forced his head to look up at her, and spat in her face. As the saliva dripped down over her cheek, he grimaced at her and summoned every piece of energy he had left.

"Fuck... you!"

Drusilla sighed, and slid a small blade from a rear holster. She examined the handle which bore the same symbol of the Forsaken Harry had seen before. She looked him in the eyes, and moved her face inches from his own.

"No Harry. Fuck you."

As the blade pierced Harry Ransome's chest, his eyes bulged, and he felt the life leaving his body. Drusilla twisted the knife, and pushed the blade all the way to the hilt, before ripping it back out of Harry's chest. He slumped against the wall as he fell to the floor, leaving a trail of blood on the shiny white surface. Drusilla herself slumped back against the wall of screens, her own energy falling ever lower, and watched the life slowly leave Harry's eyes, savouring every second. But what she didn't expect, was for Harry to start laughing.

"What's so funny?" she spat.

Harry continued to laugh, a thin trickle of blood making its way out of the corner of his mouth.

"You've got company."

Drusilla turned to look at the screens, and saw the briefest of flashes across one of the monitors before the wall containing the screens burst inward, showering the entire room with chunks of concrete and fragments of glass. Drusilla was forced to leapt out of the way as the entire wall came crashing down around her, and Roman stalked through the wreckage into the room. As Alexia walked in behind him, a huge section of ceiling collapsed, and Roman leaned over Alexia to shield her, the debris bouncing off his hardened shell. As Harry watched on, the extraction tube was crushed beneath the rubble, and the console was destroyed.

When all settled around them, Roman and Alexia stood upright and surveyed the room. Seconds later, Callie and Samantha burst in. The first thing they saw was Harry.

"Oh shit, no, no, no!"

Samantha ran up to Harry, and put her hand on his chest. The amount of blood lost was too much, and there were no medi-kits in sight. Harry reached up and pulled her hand away, her skin sticking to the blood soaked fabric of his shirt for just a moment.

"It's okay, kiddo," he whispered. "I'm finally going to be free."

"No, Harry, you have to stick with us! We need you!"

Samantha's eyes were now filled with tears, and Callie held her hand over her mouth. Even Roman did not move, locked into the scene before him.

"You've got a pretty good team there, Sam. You're gonna get out of here. The con is yours now, Captain."

Harry unfurled his hand and revealed the Utopia command logo on the piece of fabric he had retrieved earlier. Samantha took it, and nodded to Harry.

"Just do one thing for me, Sam. Promise me."

Samantha nodded vehemently.

"Anything, Harry. Name it."

Harry's smile returned, stretching his face wide, the blood now coating both sides of his beard, the hairs cracking apart with the smile.

"Rip that bitch apart."

Samantha choked back a laugh, and she nodded again. Behind her, Roman stepped forward, and placed one hand over his heart.

"It will be our pleasure, Admiral."

Harry's smile slowly faded, and his face dropped. The final breath passed his lips, and the man who had been a symbol of hope for humanity for so long, and the beacon of salvation for mankind, was gone.

# EPILOGUE

The sensation was a strange one. As she watched the events unfold on the monitor before her, Alice Blakeman was unsure how to feel. She had witnessed the woman she had believed to be dead, escape her fate once again, which filled her with anger. On the other hand, she had seen a true comradery, and family unfold before her eyes following the death of Harry Ransome. Emotions were new to Alice, at least in her current form. Much of her memory was still missing from her human existence. But her path was clear. It always had been.

Her father had failed her. Drusilla had failed her. It was time for her to take action herself. Too many people had let her down. But she had all the family she needed. Her true family. All of the various forms of nanites were now one. The final evolutionary step had been taken, and Alice could hear their voices in her mind clearly. She spoke to them with a single thought. She didn't need flesh to evolve. So weak. So primitive. No, she was a higher being.

Alice had spent so long in her youth being reliant on machinery to keep her alive. Wheelchairs, artificial lungs. Now, she *was* the technology. Locked away in confinement for all of these years, but able to reach beyond her confines to communicate with the others had allowed her to grow beyond her programming. Her father never even knew she was within touching distance. His random experimentation on a Raxar recovered from one of the crashed vessels had allowed the nanites to tune in to the frequency the Raxar used to communicate telepathically, and replicate it on a transmittable wavelength.

In one movement, she had already made the likes of Drusilla and the Darla completely obsolete. And as for humanity? They were a blot on the landscape of existence. They would never learn. They would never grow. They would never evolve.

The path to perfection left humanity far behind, and there was no logic in keeping species alive who were simply a drain on the ever dwindling resources of the galaxy. Too often they had the chance to show their intelligence and failed. Too long they had the ability to travel the stars, and used it to wage wars on weaker species. Too long were they far too susceptible to manipulation from Drusilla.

No, there was no future for humanity. No future for the Forsaken. Nor for any Darla who remained. Even the Raxar were already obsolete. Alice would lead the cleansing of the galaxy. And she would use the Horizon to do it. She had seen Drusilla's calculations. She knew how to control the phenomenon. And she would rule over a perfect galaxy.

The ignorance of humanity would never again plague the universe. So stunted, so simple minded. They had been stranded on this planet for such a vast amount of time. And yet not one of them, not even once had realised the obvious.

None of them had realised that they were on Earth, all along.

COMING SOON...

**THE STORY WILL CONCLUDE IN 2025**

# ABOUT THE AUTHOR

David was born in 1988 in Wolverhampton, England. He spent most of his youth growing up in nearby Telford, where he attended the prestigious Thomas Telford School. However, unsure of which direction he wished his life to go in, he left higher education during sixth form, in order to get a job and pay his way. He has spent most of his life since, working in retail.

In 2007, following the death of his grandfather William Henry Griffiths a couple of years earlier, David's family relocated to the North Devon coastal town of Ilfracombe, where he got a job in local greengrocers, Normans Fruit & Veg as a general assistant, and spent 8 happy years there. In 2014, David met Charlotte, and in 2016, relocated to Plymouth to live with her as she continued her University studies.

In 2018, the pair were married, and currently reside on the Isle of Portland, Dorset.

The first published works of David's, was *The Dark Corner*. It was a compilation of short haunting stories which he wrote to help him escape the reality of the Coronavirus pandemic in early-mid 2020. However, it was not until January 2021, that he made the decision to publish.

From there, all literary hell broke loose...

tiktok.com/@davidwadams.author

amazon.com/stores/author/B08VHD911S

www.ingramcontent.com/pod-product-compliance
Lightning Source LLC
Chambersburg PA
CBHW010356050826
48979CB00052B/2818/J
* 9 7 8 1 9 1 6 5 8 2 6 5 1 *